KNIT ONE, HEIST ONE

Also by Donna Moore

The Devil's Draper
The Unpicking
Old Dogs
Go to Helena Handbasket

DONNA MOORE

KNIT ONE, HEIST ONE

NO EXIT PRESS

First published in the UK in 2026 by No Exit Press,
an imprint of Bedford Square Publishers Ltd,
London, UK

noexit.co.uk
@noexitpress

A Maxim Jakubowski book

A CIP catalogue record for this book is available from the British Library.

ISBN
978-1-83501-465-3 (Paperback)
978-1-83501-466-0 (eBook)

2 4 6 8 10 9 7 5 3 1

Typeset in 10.8 on 13.5pt Garamond MT Pro
by Avocet Typeset, Bideford, Devon, EX39 2BP
Printed and bound in Great Britain by
CPI Group (UK) Ltd, Croydon CR0 4YY

FSC www.fsc.org
MIX
Paper | Supporting responsible forestry
FSC® C013604

The manufacturer's authorised representative in the EU for product safety is Easy Access System Europe, Mustamäe tee 50, 10621 Tallinn, Estonia
gpsr.requests@easproject.com

To my mum, Joyce, who lives in a retirement community which is almost nothing like Janus Lodge. Almost.

1

'FOUR AND TWO, FORTY-TWO... SEVEN AND NINE, seventy-nine...' Sylvia Abercrombie gave a deep sigh and spun her wheelchair expertly around to face the door. She couldn't bear to be in that sad room with its game of Death Bingo a moment longer. The little squares of dancing brightness from the huge glitterball in the middle of the ceiling and the cheery sunshine yellow of the walls did nothing to lift her mood. Besides, if she had to watch Effie McCallum in her winceyette goonie and curlers prancing up to the front to pick up yet another prize, she wouldn't be able to hold her tongue. The woman had the luck of the Devil. Sylvia tucked her own turquoise fleece dressing gown more closely around herself and started to wheel herself over to the door.

'Legs... eleven.' The lugubrious voice of Archie Stark was drowned out by a chorus of half-hearted whistles. Sylvia smacked the big metal button that opened the automatic doors to Janus Lodge's function suite. 'Two and three, twenty-three.'

'House!'

Even if Sylvia hadn't recognised the cackling voice, the accusatory whispers around the room would have given it away. Archie's voice held a hint of disapproval. 'Well done yet again, Effie, hen. That's a wee tin of gravy granules for Effie, there. Now, we're on the pink card, ladies and gents. Eyes down, look in. Individual sachet of custard powder for a line; jar of mint sauce for a full house.'

The doors closed smoothly behind Sylvia and she set her chair to top speed. She didn't need to worry about bumping into anyone as she made her way through the chicane of walkers and mobility scooters that lined the corridor to the front door. It was three in the morning, after all, and the few residents who weren't asleep were in the function suite playing Death Bingo. In her twelve years at Janus Lodge, Sylvia had never quite understood the desire to play a game of bingo following the death of a resident. She didn't even know how most of them knew there *had* been a death. Her own apartment was on the side nearest the driveway and she was a light sleeper, so she always heard the sirens out on the main road. Out of courtesy, the ambulances generally switched them off when they turned into the long driveway, but she heard them as they came to a screeching halt outside. Then the doors of the ambulance slammed, followed by the clatter of the paramedics as they barged through the front doors.

Sylvia was surprised that some of the residents heard *anything* with their hearing aids out and over their own rumbling snores. Yet most of them managed to emerge from their apartments – rubbing sleep from their eyes and putting their teeth in – and wander dozily and unsteadily to the function room, looking like a band of decrepit quilted zombies walking through the hallways of the damned in a nightmarish Damart advert. Somehow, their finely tuned senses could feel the approach of death. Janus Lodge was death's waiting room, after all, and none of its residents were very far away from being called in for that final appointment.

The front door was propped open and delicate fingers of mist made their way over the threshold, only to be swallowed up by the heat blasting from the radiators that lined the walls. Lydia Wheelan, Janus Lodge's live-in manager, listener, lightbulb-changer and referee, hopped from foot to foot on the wide driveway, shivering in the early morning cold. She had wrapped her arms around herself and, at first glance, it looked as though she was being hugged by someone wearing an identical green and purple tartan suit to the one she had on. No matter what time of the day or night, Lydia was always impeccably turned out in her official Janus Lodge uniform. Sylvia took a detour into Lydia's office and plucked a multicoloured, woollen shawl from the back of the door, placing it on her lap as she wheeled herself outside into the chilly air.

She stopped for a moment to take in the scene. The Douglas firs which lined the driveway swayed gently and, in the distance, a band of mist separated the snow-capped hills from the heather and bracken which clung to the hillside. The ground frost sparkled in the glow of the ambulance's slowly turning blue light. If it wasn't for the ambulance and the body on the stretcher being loaded gently into it by two paramedics, the scene was peaceful and reassuring. Sylvia could almost imagine a lone piper appearing out of nowhere to treat them to a mournful rendition of 'Amazing Grace'.

She wheeled herself over to Lydia and handed her the shawl, squeezing her arm as she did so. Lydia looked down at her, her face strained and tear-streaked. 'Thanks, Sylvia.' She wrapped the shawl around herself, further dislodging the bun which had once been neat and smooth but which was now hanging in wispy strands over her face. She stroked the soft wool and her lip trembled. She nodded her head towards the ambulance. 'It was Jessie who made this for me, you know.'

Sylvia ran her fingers over the fringes of the shawl. 'Aye, hen. She'll be missed, eh?'

'She will indeed, Sylvia. She was a lovely wee woman, so she was.'

'Aye. Always had the kettle on the go. And never once, in all the years I've been here, did she fail to give ye a wee bit of her home-made shortbread when she had you round for a brew. Never would give me the recipe, though.'

Lydia smiled and put a hand on Sylvia's shoulder. 'Yes, she was always so generous with that shortbread.'

'Not like some of these old bastards in here.'

'Sylvia!'

'Well, some of them wouldn't even give ye a foosty old Rich Tea biscuit and a wee dunk of a week-old teabag.'

Lydia shook her head and leaned down to give Sylvia an awkward hug. 'You really are incorrigible.'

Sylvia patted Lydia's hand as it lay on the arm of her chair. 'I'm right though, doll, eh? They *are* a miserable shower.' They watched in silence as the ambulance slowly pulled away and drove down the long, winding drive. Halfway down, the blue light went off. Lydia sighed and drew the shawl more closely around her. Sylvia shivered. 'Cold enough to freeze the balls off ye. You should get home, love, or at least get inside. I'm away back to the bingo. Somebody's got to check on that Effie McCallum. I think she's sold her soul to the Devil for a packet of blancmange and a jar of Lidl's own-brand mint sauce.'

'I'll be in in a minute, Sylvia.' Lydia lifted her shoulders to her ears as though to ease off the tension and continued to stare after the disappearing ambulance. Sylvia spun her wheelchair to face the doors. Over the front of the building was a large gold and black sign, proclaiming it to be 'Janus Lodge – Retirement Apartments for the Young at Heart', with an accompanying image of a bearded Roman god with two faces looking in opposite directions.

'Jeez-o.' Sylvia stopped short and put a hand to her chest. Behind the familiar tattered posters with their peeling Sellotape – warning residents to be vigilant about strangers, bogus callers and speeding mobility scooters – a malevolent statue stared out at the two women. It could have been the immobile, stony face of Janus himself. Sylvia turned back to Lydia. 'Bloody hell, doll. I don't blame you for wanting to stay out here, despite the cold. Have you seen what's waiting for you?'

Lydia turned round and sighed when she saw the face at the window. 'Oh dear. It's Gregor. I wonder what he wants. He doesn't look very happy, does he?'

Sylvia snorted. 'Never bloody does. Christ on a bike. I hope Jessie didnae see that face of his afore she died. She'd have thought it was the Grim Reaper come to personally escort her to the other side.'

Lydia bit back a laugh. 'Now, now, Sylvia. That's no way to talk about him, is it?'

'How no'? After all, I was married to the old misery for forty-odd years. I think I earned the bloody right to talk about him however I like.' She glowered at the unmoving Gregor. 'Jeez-o. Look at him. Here's the rest of us in our dressing gowns and slippers, and he's suited and booted and wearing a freshly laundered shirt and black tie at three in the morning. He probably goes to bed in them, just in case one of us dies, the old ghoul. We should start calling him Nosferatu.' She shook her head and turned back to Lydia. 'Good luck, hen. You'll need it, by the look of that sour face.' With that, Sylvia wheeled herself through the door. As she reached Gregor he pointedly turned away, and she stuck her tongue out at his back before unlocking her apartment door. She couldn't help childishness overtaking her whenever she saw him. Inside, she pushed the door to, but left it slightly ajar, cocking her head to catch the conversation outside her flat.

She could hear Lydia sighing as she returned inside, the outside door closing softly behind her. 'Did you want to see me, Mr Abercrombie? Are you off up to the bingo?' Sylvia grinned. Gregor would love that one.

Gregor snorted. 'Not bloody likely. Stupid idea. Playing bingo when someone dies.'

'Some of the residents find it… a comfort.' Lydia's voice was artificially bright.

'Not me. It's no' normal. Bunch of freaks.'

Lydia sighed. 'Anyway, can I do something to help you, Mr Abercrombie?'

His voice was abrupt and to the point. 'Was that Jessie McNish that they just took away in that ambulance?'

Lydia's voice trembled. 'I'm afraid it was, yes.'

'Is she dead?'

There was a pause before Lydia answered. 'Sadly, yes.'

'So she's definitely no' coming back, then?'

Lydia's voice was sharper than Sylvia had ever heard it before. 'No, Mr Abercrombie, she's definitely not coming back. I'm aware that medical science has advanced, but not *that* much, I'm afraid.' Then, obviously relenting, her voice softened. 'I'm really sorry, I didn't mean to be rude. This morning has been rather a strain for all of us, hasn't it?'

Sylvia knew what Gregor was going to say before the words were out of his mouth. 'Has it?'

Lydia, however, seemed taken aback by his response. 'Well… yes. Jessie was… It's very… Look, what is it that I can help you with, Mr Abercrombie?'

'I saw the ambulance men loading the stretcher and just wanted to see how Jessie was. I knew she wasn't well, so I've been keeping an eye on her.' Sylvia couldn't believe what she was hearing. Gregor had never shown the slightest bit of care and concern for anyone. Not since… well, not since before…

It was best not to think about that. Sylvia gently opened the door a smidgeon more and positioned herself so she could see what was happening. Lydia looked as surprised as Sylvia felt. 'You have? That was… nice of you. I'm so sorry; I didn't realise that you and Jessie were close.'

Gregor rocked back on his heels. 'Close? What do you mean, close? I hardly knew the woman.'

A look of confusion crossed Lydia's face. 'Then… I don't… I'm afraid I don't understand, Mr Abercrombie.'

'Her flat.' He crossed his arms. Lydia shook her head, clearly confused. Sylvia, however, knew exactly what Gregor meant and had to stop herself from going out there and knocking him over with her wheelchair. 'Her *flat*. For God's sake, woman. It's bigger than mine and I'm putting my name down for it before anyone else does. I knew she was ill, so I've been watching her, waiting for this opportunity.'

'Oppor…?' Lydia gave him a disgusted look, turned on her heel and went into her office, shutting the door firmly behind her.

Sylvia slowly and quietly closed her own door as Gregor continued his conversation with the empty hallway. 'I *am* first, right? Nobody else has claimed it yet, have they?' His voice was gradually increasing in volume and annoyance. 'I got in first, that apartment's mine. My name's been down for a bigger one since the day I moved in, Ms Wheelan, don't you forget that. I've been waiting for a whole year for that flat.' As Gregor stomped back up the corridor, Sylvia heard him kicking over the cheery gnome outside her neighbour's door. 'Hormones. Bloody women. I'd better get that flat or there'll be trouble.' Sylvia shook her head and wheeled herself into her living room. There was no chance of sleep, now. She'd watch *Nightmare Alley*. It was bleak, but it always cheered her up.

2

The silver Mercedes S-Class, its windows tinted to hide its occupants, purred into the car park and drove around before finally pulling into a space marked 'CEO'. The space was directly at the front of the building – a shiny glass, brass and marble affair. Over the door was an elaborate sign saying 'Prometheus Holdings' in gold and red, with the image of a large flame behind it.

The front passenger door opened almost before the car had come to a halt and a short, skinny young man, his face covered in angry, red spots, jumped out of the car and ran around to the driver's-side door. The legs of his blue and white tracksuit bottoms brushed together with a rustle of static as he scurried around the car. He opened the door and stepped back to let out a man in his fifties, wearing a smart cashmere coat and black leather gloves. The man was trim, with closely cropped grey hair and tanned, carefully moisturised skin. Had it not been for the rather nasty chib mark giving him a ragged smile from ear to chin, he would have looked like a particularly well-paid bank manager. Dennis 'Grinder' Mahoney was, indeed, well-paid, but more prone to robbing banks than managing them.

One of the back doors of the Mercedes slowly opened and the car dipped to one side. Mahoney nodded at the young man in the tracksuit who was now standing next to him, waiting expectantly. 'PJ, help Declan out.' PJ put his arm into the car and a meaty hand grabbed hold of it. After a few moments of struggle, a second tracksuited man stepped out. His tracksuit, however, fitted a little more snugly than PJ's. Declan looked like a man who spent twenty-three hours a day down the gym – three of them working out and the other twenty taking steroids. He stood for a moment to catch his breath and Mahoney surveyed them both, a look of disgust on his face, before striding off towards the office building.

PJ immediately ran after his boss and managed to arrive at the building's doors just in time to open them for Mahoney, who entered without thanking his minion. PJ clearly didn't expect any thanks. Declan lumbered slowly after them both, breathing loudly through his mouth, and turning sideways to fit through the door.

The reception area of Prometheus Holdings was entirely cold, sterile marble. A smartly dressed young man was sitting behind the wide marble reception desk that rose seamlessly out of the matching floor, a Bluetooth device flashing in his ear. He looked up and smiled professionally as Mahoney entered. The smile faltered a little as his eyes took in PJ and Declan behind their boss. 'May I help you… gentlemen?'

Mahoney simply kept walking towards the bank of lifts at the far end of the vast reception area, not even bothering to look at the young man as he answered. 'Naw, pal, you're alright. We're here to see Fergus Lamont.'

The receptionist stood up, looking puzzled. This wasn't how things were done at Prometheus Holdings. He called after the three visitors. 'Excuse me, sir. Is Mr Lamont expecting you?'

The response was offhand. 'He will be, pal, aye… when he sees me.'

The receptionist looked after them, his mouth open, as they stepped into the lift. He picked up the phone and dialled a number as the doors shut.

Mahoney, PJ and Declan stepped out of the lift at the top floor and into an office foyer that was smart, minimalist and empty apart from a desk holding a fancy flatscreen computer and a phone. The phone was buzzing tastefully but insistently. A name plate at the front of the desk read 'Miss Jodie Wilde'. 'Looks as though Miss Wilde has stepped away from her desk, lads.' Mahoney flicked an invisible speck of dust off his cashmere coat. 'You'd better answer that phone, PJ. Sounds important.'

PJ nodded and picked up the receiver. He listened for a moment. 'Aye, nae worries, wee man, we managed to find our own way up in the lift.' He put the receiver back down. 'That wee nyaff at reception. Sounds like he was worried about us.' The phone started to buzz again. PJ picked it up with a sigh. 'Naw, she's still no' here. An' ah'm still no' yer secretary.' He put the receiver down on the desk and the faint bleating of a frantic voice echoed tinnily on the shiny desktop.

Mahoney gestured to the closed walnut door that stood in front of them. PJ walked over and turned the shiny brass handle without knocking. As they entered the room, a voluptuous redhead rushed past them, looking slightly dishevelled and pulling down the hem of her short skirt. 'That fanny down on reception was looking for ye,' PJ told her helpfully, closing the door firmly behind her.

The office was large and plush, clad in walnut and containing all the trappings of a successful business. A huge picture window looked out over the nearby loch and mountains. The glorious view, however, was wasted on the man who sat at his desk with his back to the window. Right now, he was red-faced and blinking as he adjusted the crotch of his trousers. His face paled when he saw Mahoney.

Mahoney's voice was pleasant. 'Not busy, I hope, Fergus?'

Fergus Lamont pouted. 'Well, actually…'

'Good, good. Wouldn't have liked to have interrupted you in the middle of something urgent.'

'We were… ah…'

'Dictation, it looked like, Fergus, if I'm not mistaken.' Mahoney took off his coat and held it up between two fingers without looking round. PJ dashed over and took it from him, reverently, and hung it up on a coat stand in the corner of the room. Mahoney looked Fergus up and down and his nose wrinkled. 'Nice suit, Fergus. I once saw similar on sale at Paddy's Market.'

Lamont bristled. 'Actually, Grinder, it's an Armani.'

'Is it, aye? Ah, well, it doesn't suit you. You look like mutton dressed as Osso Bucco.' Mahoney took off his leather gloves and placed them carefully on Fergus's desk, before sitting down, equally carefully pulling up the legs of his trousers as he did so. He crossed his legs, resting one smart and highly polished shoe on the opposite knee. 'Now, I have a wee business proposition for you, Fergus.'

Fergus Lamont lost the grumpy look on his face and spread his arms, expansively. 'Of course, Grinder, you know I'm always happy to do business with a man such as yourself. Which part of my empire can be of assistance this time?'

'Well, as it happens, Fergus, I'm thinking of opening a… shall we say… a high-class gentlemen's club.'

'You mean a broth—?'

Mahoney raised a warning hand. 'Aye, Fergus, I mean a high-class gentlemen's club, as I said.'

'Of course, of course. Branching out from bookies and bingo then, Grinder?' His visitor stared pointedly at him and Lamont hurried on. 'Anyway, how can I help you with this exactly?'

Mahoney inspected his nails. 'Well, you manage those bingo halls and bookies so well for me that I thought I'd offer you a wee partnership in this new venture.' Lamont gave a self-satisfied smile and puffed out his chest. One side of Mahoney's mouth twisted upwards, as though the idea of managing an entire smile was below him. The scar on his face whitened with the effort. 'Besides, you have just the perfect spot of land on your books for the purpose.'

Lamont looked puzzled. 'I do?'

'Indeed. Slightly out of town, quiet setting… nowhere the neighbours are likely to complain. I've already managed to… persuade, shall we say… my contact on the City Council that this will go through planning without a hitch.' He laughed, mirthlessly. 'Not that he had much choice, eh, lads?'

PJ grunted a sycophantic laugh. 'Naw, boss, no' really.'

Mahoney removed his highly polished foot from his knee and leaned forward, his forearms resting on the table and his perfectly manicured hands clasped in front of him. 'Mind you, Fergus, the Planning Department aren't yet aware that they've already passed this one, so this is strictly hush-hush for the time being, if you don't mind.'

Lamont's face still had its puzzled look. 'I won't say a word, Grinder. But… well, I think you're mistaken.' He tapped a few keys on his computer. 'Aye, you must have got it wrong. I've got a couple of plots of land in the portfolio, but both of them are city centre locations, nothing out of town.' He turned the screen towards Mahoney. 'This one would have been perfect – it was that very profitable homeless hostel they made me pull down, but it's already been earmarked for multistorey parking, so if that's the one you're thinking of, you're too late, sadly.' He twisted the screen back towards himself. 'Not to say that there isn't something suitable out there, though. I can always scout around for you on the quiet, if that would help? For a small finder's fee, of course.' He sat back in his chair and beamed at his visitor.

Mahoney shook his head. 'No need, Fergus. I told you, you've already got the perfect spot for it, something a wee bit more upmarket, in a nice quiet area with some space around it. Perfect for a high-class establishment like mine.' He stood up and moved swiftly around the desk. He took the computer mouse out of Lamont's hand, looked at the screen and smoothly navigated to the page he was looking for. 'There. That's the one I'm talking about.' He straightened up and returned to his seat.

Fergus stared at the screen and then looked back at Mahoney's satisfied face, shaking his head. 'But that's—'

'I know what it is, Fergus. But I want to knock it down and build—'

'A brothel.'

Mahoney sat forward and tapped a manicured fingernail on the desk. 'A high-class *gentlemen's* club.'

3

THE COMMUNAL LOUNGE OF JANUS LODGE WAS large, bright and cheerful, with a comfortable, distinctly lived-in look. Light poured in through the large windows and the walls were hung with photographs and paintings. Some of the paintings were faded reproductions of Old Masters, others had been painted by the residents. The latter varied in quality but had been given pride of place. The room was an obstacle course of comfortable but unmatched chairs with high backs and sturdy arms, and strategically placed side tables.

Knitted objects in a riot of colours covered every available surface, making the room look as though there had been an explosion in a wool factory. Every chair had a brightly coloured blanket thrown over it and its arms were protected by knitted armrests – sometimes matching, more often not. Every chair contained at least two fat, knitted cushions and crocheted doilies covered every available flat surface. Even the ancient organ in the corner had a knitted cover, and its legs were resplendent in multicoloured woollen legwarmers, in a show of Victorian prudery mixed with *Kids from Fame* exuberance.

This morning, the large room only held three residents. Sylvia was sitting in her wheelchair in front of the fire, flanked, as usual, by two of her dearest friends, Francine Ure and Nettie Forbes. Francine was as unlike Sylvia as it was possible to get. Where Sylvia was tiny and round, with hair the colour of a ripe tomato, Francine was tall, slim and elegant. She always reminded Sylvia of Katherine Hepburn at her sternest. Nettie, slightly younger than Sylvia and Francine, in her late seventies, was soft and cushiony, with a matching face, as though its creator had been asked to draw the ideal grandma. Unlike the other two, Nettie was still in her nightclothes and a floor-length towelling dressing gown and slippers.

The three women were knitting in companionable silence, surrounded by large bags full of balls of wool, needles and patterns. Sylvia was crocheting a large, delicate doily shaped like a butterfly, multicoloured and beautiful. From time to time, she held it up to check its progress. Each time she did, Nettie looked at it enviously; her own simple baby-blue blanket looked lumpy and amateurish beside the work of her friends. She sighed and continued knitting laboriously, her tongue poking out of the side of her mouth as she concentrated. Francine was working on a complicated Fair Isle sweater with at least ten different colours of wool and an intricate pattern. Her wool bag was spewing wool that, to the untrained eye – Sylvia glanced at Nettie – would look like a tangle of multicoloured spaghetti, but which quickly and effortlessly transformed itself into a work of art in Francine's talented care. Sylvia had never said anything to her friends but even she envied Francine her knitting prowess.

Occasionally, Francine and Nettie would pause to take a sip of tea from the delicate china cups sitting on the knitted doilies on the tables next to them. Other than that, the industrious clacking of needles was undisturbed until the sound of heavy footsteps and the rattling of buckles could be heard in the corridor outside. Sylvia looked at her watch and smiled happily. 'Ooooh, here's Jake.' Nettie patted her hair in readiness and Francine put her knitting to one side. Sylvia's grandson was a firm favourite with all of them.

Jake loped into the lounge, motorbike helmet in hand. His leather and tattoos looked out of place amidst the fluffy decor, but he obviously felt at home. 'Mornin', ladies. Called at your place, Gran, and when there was no answer, I knew I'd find you in here. Either here or down at Shawfield, losing my inheritance on the dogs.' His voice was a Tom Waits growl. The three women nodded and smiled at him as he kissed Sylvia gently on the cheek. 'Mornin', Gran. You're lookin' lovely today. That colour hair suits you. I prefer it to the orange you did for Halloween.'

Sylvia patted her fiery red hair, looking pleased with herself. 'Morning, love. How's it hanging?' Francine raised her eyebrows at Nettie, who giggled behind her hand.

Jake crossed to Francine and kissed the top of her head, and did the same with Nettie. Nettie giggled girlishly once again and Jake chucked her under the chin. 'Good to see three of my favourite ladies looking so sprightly.' He looked around the room. 'Bit quiet in here today, isn't it?'

Francine smiled at him. 'Second Tuesday in the month.' Jake looked blankly at her. 'It's Tech Club.'

Jake's face was still blank. He shook his head. 'What's Tech Club?'

Sylvia frowned down at her butterfly as her crochet needle flew. 'Well, it's Tech Club, isn't it?'

Jake's eyebrows furrowed as he looked at his grandmother, then his face cleared. 'Oh! I see!' He tapped the side of his nose. 'I presume that the first rule of Tech Club is that you don't talk about Tech Club?'

Sylvia finished her row and put her crochet aside. 'What *are* you talking about, Jake?'

As she looked up at him, he grinned down at her. 'Treat me as though I'm five years old. What's Tech Club?'

Sylvia waved a vague hand. 'It's Harriet's baby. She started it a couple of months ago because people kept asking her questions. If people have problems with their… tech… then they take it along to Tech Club and Harriet sorts it out for them. You know…' She waved her hand again, as if that explained everything. 'If the messages aren't getting through, or the… internet's dead or something…'

'Like some sort of seance, you mean?' Jake carried on hurriedly as Sylvia scowled at him. 'Anyway, it sounds as though *you* could benefit from Tech Club. Why aren't you there?'

'Don't be ridiculous, Jake. I'm not like the rest of these old biddies in here.' Francine and Nettie exchanged another look. 'What do I want with Tech Club?'

Jake gazed at her. 'Well, last week when I came to see you, I had to close about three hundred open tabs on your iPad, and last time I video-called you on WhatsApp all I could see of you was the top of your head.'

Sylvia snorted. 'You know I don't like that zipzap thing; I prefer it when you're here in person.' She patted the empty chair next to her. 'Now, sit down and give us news of the outside world.'

As he settled himself in their midst, Francine reached out a liver-spotted hand and stroked it against his rough skin. 'Ooh, Jake, lovey, your face is so cold. You should have wrapped up better.' Her diction was precise and perfectly modulated.

Sylvia tucked her crochet away in her capacious home-made knitting bag. 'Your da okay, son?'

'Aye, he's fine – sends his love.' Jake put his motorbike helmet on the table and rubbed his hands together, blowing on his fingers to warm them up. 'It's bloody freezin' out. Lovely and warm in here, but.'

'Aye, of course it is. This place is on permanent Gobi Desert setting.' It was one of Sylvia's pet peeves. 'If this lot did more than sit on their arses all day… sorry, Francine… it wouldn't need to be up so high. These old fogies don't give a toss about climate change.'

Jake unzipped his leather jacket, revealing a bright, striped scarf. 'Francine, this scarf you knitted for me is a stoater. How are you at knitting balaclavas? Be nice to have one for under my helmet, this time of year.'

Francine beamed. 'Of course, my dear boy. What colour do you want?'

'Eh… no' sure… blue, mibbee? That be okay?' She nodded happily and he leaned over and gave her another kiss. 'You're a gem, Frankie, doll.'

Sylvia hid a smile. No one but Jake could get away with calling Francine 'Frankie, doll'. She made a mental note to try it one day and see how she fared.

Francine made as if to stand. 'Would you like a cup of tea, Jake?'

He gestured her to sit back down, fluffing up the cushion behind her back as he did so. 'Naw. Just dropped in to give Gran a message from Dad, and a wee pick-me-up.'

Sylvia looked at him in anticipation at the comment and Jake turned to her, reaching into the pockets of his leather jacket. From each one he took a can of Guinness, which he put down on the little table next to Sylvia.

She blew a kiss at him, opened one of the cans with a sigh of pleasure and took a long gulp. She smacked her lips and wiped her mouth on the sleeve of her thick hand-knitted cardigan. 'Ah, that's hit the spot. Nice and cold, too. That's braw. Cheers, Jake. Now, what's your dad saying?'

'He's gonnae pick you up to go shopping on Thursday, Gran, as usual. An' he says why don't you leave that bloody mobile on. His words, no' mine.'

Sylvia took another swig and wiped more froth from her mouth. 'Och, I don't like they mobile phones; I read somewhere that they can irradiate you and make you impotent. Ah'm no' wanting to be irradiated, and I'm definitely no' wantin' to be impotent. That would never do.'

Francine rapped Sylvia's knuckles with her knitting needles, an ineffectual move, since on Jake's arrival Francine had stuck them into one of her enormous balls of wool.

Jake snorted. 'That's really too much information, Gran. Christ, I feel sick now. Didn't need to know that, I really didn't.'

Nettie shook her head, dropping several stitches as she did so but completely oblivious to the fact. 'I swear, I've never met anyone who has such peculiar ideas as you, Sylvia. Where on earth do you get them from?'

Sylvia took another glug from the can of Guinness and carried on as if she hadn't noticed the interruptions. 'Mind you, might be an improvement, being irradiated. I hear it tightens the skin.'

Jake laughed and kissed his gran again. 'Right, I'd better get back. It's alright for you ladies of leisure, but some of us have to work. See you three gorgeous dollybirds later.'

Sylvia snorted. 'Dollybirds? More like the three witches, ya cheeky wee sh—'

'Sylvia!'

'Whoops, sorry, Francine.'

Jake left the room and they could hear his laugh ringing out as he walked down the corridor.

Francine put the sweater she had been knitting to one side and rummaged in her knitting bag. 'Oh dear – all these colours and I haven't got any blue wool for Jake's balaclava.' She looked over at Nettie's knitting bag lying on the floor next to her chair, spewing multiple balls of baby-blue wool.

Nettie sighed and put down her own knitting. She groaned as she bent down and pushed the bag over towards Francine. 'Here, have this. It's better in your hands than mine, anyway. To be honest, I'm sick of the sight of the stuff; I'm never going to be rid of it all.'

Sylvia looked at the little pile of badly knitted blue blankets on the floor next to Nettie, destined for the maternity unit at the hospital. 'Why in holy hell are all your baby blankets pale blue, anyway? What if there's a rush of wee girl babies born? They're going to be fuc—' Francine cleared her throat. 'Sorry, doll. They're going to be *bloody* freezing.'

Nettie picked a piece of the offending wool off her lap. 'It's Sally, my daughter. I told her I liked this colour once and she keeps bringing me them from her shop. I haven't got the heart to tell her I've still got two hundred balls of it in the wardrobe.'

4

Grinder Mahoney was smiling and his voice was pleasant, but there was menace not far beneath the surface. Fergus Lamont shivered; he'd seen the consequences of Grinder using that voice before. PJ and Declan moved a step closer, just to reinforce the message in case Lamont didn't quite get it. Lamont shook his head. 'But that's where…'

Mahoney gave his cold smile again. 'I will, of course, make it worth your while, Fergus. I was thinking… two and a half million?'

Lamont narrowed his eyes, calculating the potential benefits and drawbacks. 'But that place is a nice little earner for me, Grinder. The rents are always paid on time and there's never any trouble. Besides, I couldn't let you have it anyway. It's where my parents live, and my grandfather inserted a clause in the deeds to the place before he died… The miserable old bastard.'

'What sort of a clause?'

Lamont pouted. 'Some sort of Right of First Refusal or some such. By the time my grandfather died, Dad was already beginning to show signs of… well, odd behaviour. Let's just say… he's a bit senile, and my mother was happy just to go along with it. There was no way Dad could have taken over the business. So, grandfather had to leave it to me…' He gazed thoughtfully at nothing for a few moments. 'But he didn't like me very much for some reason…' Mahoney raised an eyebrow, as if to show that this revelation wasn't a complete shock to him, and Lamont hurriedly continued. 'Anyway, he put in a clause that says that my parents have to be looked after at Janus Lodge for as long as they live. And, even after they're gone, the old farts who live there must be offered first refusal on any sale.'

Mahoney nodded. 'Look, I'm not ungenerous, Fergus. I want that land. Let's just call it a nice round three million, shall we? I'm sure the… old farts… won't be able to compete with that, will they?'

A pitter-pattering started somewhere in Lamont's chest. Three million? If Mahoney was happy to go up to three million so easily, then perhaps he could be persuaded even higher. There might be a way around the deed; he'd get his lawyer onto it. 'Well…'

'Excellent.' Mahoney stuck out his hand and Lamont took it automatically. 'We have a deal, then. Now, let's sort out a time to go and have a look at the place, and I'll tell you my plans for it. It's going to be really high-end.' He slapped Lamont on the shoulder, all pally-pally now the business was done. 'And once it's built, there'll be a lifetime membership in the place for you. I'm sure that'll be right up your street, eh, Fergus?'

Three million wasn't to be sniffed at, but did Lamont really want to get further involved in Grinder's shady business dealings? He already knew how the man worked, and it wasn't always pleasant. Besides, the clause in his grandfather's will was pretty watertight. It wasn't as though Lamont hadn't already considered the possibilities. 'Yes… but—'

Mahoney raised a hand to stop him. 'No buts, Fergus, no buts. I might even let you have a say in the management of the place, too. After all, you've done pretty well with my bingo halls and bookies, even though you do turn your snooty wee neb up at them. It's not everyone I trust, you know.'

'I know that, Grinder, but—'

Mahoney rested his meaty hands on the desk and pushed his face towards Lamont. His hot breath smelled faintly and fairly unpleasantly of sweet, strong coffee. 'Not those nasty wee buts again, Fergus. You *do* remember what happened to your predecessor, don't you?'

PJ and Declan crossed themselves sombrely.

5

Sylvia wheeled herself along the corridor, accompanied by Jake. It was long and wide with pictures of Scottish landscapes hung at intervals. Halfway up, the hallway opened out, with big bay windows to the left and right. In the middle of the space was a small table and a notice board on a stand. The table was a repository of random treats that popped up regularly, placed there by mysterious unseen hands, although Sylvia always amused herself by guessing which resident was having a good old clear-out of wee bits of shite. These treats could be anything from an old lampshade to a box of Celebrations with only the Bounty bars left, to a 1970s magazine rack. Today's offerings were a video about East Anglian Air Ambulance and a six-pack of salt-and-vinegar Hula Hoops that was only six months out of date. She ignored the video and scooped up the Hula Hoops, tucking them swiftly into the knitting bag on her lap.

The notice board was her next focus. 'Nothing on, as usual.' Her voice dripped with disgust.

Jake stepped forward and peered at the calendar of events for the month. 'What are you talking about, Gran? There's something on every day.'

Sylvia huffed. 'Shitey wee quizzes and games of bingo? Hardly earth-shattering, is it?'

'There's Francine's Tai Chi class; you should go to that.'

Sylvia waved her arms about in front of her. 'It's all this nonsense. Cloud Hands and White Crane Spreading Wings and Spank the Monkey.'

Jake laughed. 'I'm sure there's not a Tai Chi move called Spank the Monkey.'

'Well, maybe there should be. I'd go if there was. Besides, she's too bossy. She swans in every week in that set of white pyjamas an' she takes it too seriously.'

'Is she really a black belt?'

Sylvia sighed. 'Several of them. Karate, Taekwondo, Judo… several more with names I can't pronounce. Proper Bruce Lee, she is.'

Jake nodded, impressed. 'Well, good for her, I think that's great.' He turned back to the notice board. 'What about this? That duo that was on last week. You liked them.'

Sylvia sniffed. 'Aye, well, she had a lot of go in her for a woman of seventy.' Her praise was grudging. 'But the old boy accompanying her on the harmonica was rotten.'

Not to be put off, Jake pointed at another entry. 'What's *Gentlemen's Club*?'

Sylvia glared at him. 'How would I know? I'm not a gentleman, am I? I expect they just play darts and talk. Wee Davey was the only one who turned up to it, anyway, so they're cancelling it. No, what we need are some good talks. Something interesting that'll keep our brains ticking over.'

Jake pointed at an entry in triumph. 'Here. What about this one next week: *The Hidden Stories of D-Day*? That'll be good.'

Sylvia waved a dismissive hand. 'We don't want to talk about the war all the time. They've always got us reminiscing about World War Two and singing dreary songs. Besides, what can they tell us we don't already know about?'

'Fine, Gran. I'm sorry. I had no idea that you were part of Operation Barbarossa or the sinking of the *Bismarck*.'

Sylvia ignored him. 'Mind you, we had a good talk about bees last month. I liked the talk about the bees. We were all surprised about the bees.'

'Aye? What were you surprised about?'

Sylvia turned her chair away from the notice board. 'Well, mostly we were surprised that the talk was interesting.' Jake shook his head, grinning, as they continued to make their way along the corridor.

The numbered doors on each side were brightly painted in striking gloss colours – red, turquoise, emerald, purple. Many of the flats had decorative ornaments by the side of the doors – plants in pots, ceramic cats, a red and gold Chinese dragon. Sylvia and Jake stopped outside a door flanked by a pair of stone lions and Sylvia knocked. After a few moments the door opened. Harriet Knox, a tiny, gnarled woman in her eighties, with wild grey hair and a pair of enormous thick glasses that made her eyes appear huge and bulbous, like those of a frog, peered out at them. She was leaning heavily on a stick as she held the door open. Behind her, lining every square inch of her hallway, were black-and-white photos of women playing baseball.

She smiled broadly when she saw Jake and he bent down and gave her a soft hug, as though he was frightened of snapping this tiny, brittle woman in half. 'Mornin', Harriet.'

Sylvia wheeled herself into the hallway. 'Alright, Einstein? We've come to take you for a walk, doll.' Harriet continued to smile, not registering Sylvia's words. 'I *said*… we've come to take you for a *walk*, Harriet.'

Still no reaction. Jake pointed at Harriet's ears. 'She's wearing earphones, Gran. She can't hear you.' He reached out and gently removed the earphones from Harriet's ears. 'New phone, Harriet?'

Harriet nodded, holding it up. 'iPhone 15 Pro Max. A17 Pro chip, titanium. Enormous optical zoom, three cameras, one terabyte of storage.'

'And a partridge in a pear tree,' trilled Sylvia.

Harriet ignored her and pushed her glasses further up her nose. 'I'm listening to that band you emailed me about a couple of years ago, Jake. They're still my favourites.'

Jake smiled. 'Which one?'

'Idles. I love their stuff.'

Sylvia looked at them both. 'A band? Called *Idles*? What sort of a name is that?'

Harriet pushed her glasses further up her nose. 'Really, Sylvia. You need to get a bit more with it. You'd like them; they swear a lot. Do youse want to come in? I've just put the kettle on.'

She turned to walk down the hall into the kitchen, but Sylvia reached out and stopped her. 'No, doll. Jake and I have come to take you for a walk. We haven't seen you out and about in a while. You spend too much time in front of that microwave thing.'

Harriet raised her eyebrows. 'I've told you. It's a computer. Not a microwave. Some of us use technology for more than doing jigsaw puzzles and looking for the cause of death of old film stars.'

Jake groaned. 'Tell me about it. Last time I was here you should have seen all the tabs I had to close. Along with about fourteen for Damart and a random query for "why is my cactus wonky?", she'd also been looking up the deaths of John Payne, Dean Martin, Sammy Davis Junior, Gregory Peck and Deborah Kerr. Status Quo, too, for some reason.'

'Well, I wanted to *know*. I thought that was what the cloud was for, looking things up. That's what you and your dad told me when you got it for me. Anyway, I was happy to discover that Status Quo weren't dead, so that's good, isn't it?'

Harriet pushed her glasses back up her nose. 'You should try doing other things on the computer, Sylv – it's amazing the stuff you can download.'

Sylvia looked at her blankly and then said, 'Oh, that reminds me. What does "she sells content on the website Only Fans" mean?' Jake and Harriet exchanged a horrified glance. 'It was in my newspaper. Some celebrity or other, one of those ones with the big lips. It said "she sells content on the website Only Fans". What does that mean?'

Harriet took off her glasses and polished them on the bottom of her skirt, as if playing for time. Jake cleared his throat. 'Errrr, it means she sells stuff online.'

'Oh, right. Nettie buys a lot of things off the line, but I wouldn't think that would be something worth putting in a newspaper, although, to be fair, Nettie's lips are just a normal size.'

Jake glanced at Harriet, who was still concentrating on the lenses of her glasses. 'Aye, well, I don't think it would be Only Fans Nettie gets stuff from, Gran.'

Sylvia shook her head. 'No, I think she said it was The Owl Barn.'

Jake laughed. 'Aye, that sounds much more likely.'

'She bought a lap tray with Highland cows on it and a little ornament of a mouse looking at a bluebell.' Sylvia sniffed dismissively. 'She's always buying wee bits of shite. I can't get into their flat with my chair; it would be like an episode of *It's a Knockout*, trying to negotiate all that crap.'

Harriet grinned. 'Good luck closing all her tabs after she looks up Only Fans, Jake.' Sylvia opened her mouth to speak and Harriet hurried on. 'Anyway, you two lovely people want to take me for a walk. Just let me get my coat.' She hobbled back inside and then reappeared a moment later with a thick coat. Jake helped her to put it on and they made their way slowly back down the hallway, Harriet leaning heavily on her stick, with one of Jake's meaty hands underneath her other elbow for support. All the time, Harriet kept up a steady stream of information about computers for Sylvia's benefit.

Eventually, Sylvia held up a hand. 'Listen, hen, I understand all those individual words… well, most of them, anyway… but when you put them all together they make no sense. If I need any help, I'll let you know; until then, you can keep your algorithms and your motherboards to yourself.'

As they walked out of the building, Harriet spotted Jake's motorcycle – big, meaty, shiny black and red. She limped slowly around it, stroking the gleaming chrome, peering at the dials and holding the handlebars. 'New bike, Jake?' He nodded. 'It's gorgeous.'

Sylvia tugged Jake by the sleeve. 'Take her for a ride on it, Jake.'

Harriet pointed at herself, her eyes wide behind her thick glasses and with a look of excitement and fear on her face. 'Me?'

Sylvia nodded. 'Aye, o' course you. How no'?'

'But what about this?' Harriet waved her stick, almost falling over before Jake managed to catch her. 'See? It just wouldn't work.' Her face fell.

Jake opened the pannier and took out a spare helmet, placing it firmly on Harriet's head before she could make any more excuses. He buckled the chin strap for her and stood back. 'What do you think, Gran?'

The helmet looked totally out of place, huge and awkward on Harriet's tiny little head, but Sylvia wasn't about to say that. 'Bloody brilliant. Like she was born to be in *Easy Rider*.' Sylvia handed Harriet the blanket which was covering her own knees in the wheelchair. 'Here, doll, take this.'

Harriet wrapped the blanket around herself and put on the thick leather gloves Jake handed her. She gave her stick to Sylvia to look after, leaning against Sylvia's chair to steady herself. She hesitated and then passed her mobile phone to Sylvia. 'Here, get a photo of me.'

Sylvia held the phone in two fingers as if it was something moist and unpleasant she'd picked up off the pavement. As Jake lifted Harriet onto the back of his bike and then got on himself, Harriet called out, 'It's easy. Just hold it steady then press the big round button.'

Sylvia held the phone up and closed an eye. 'I can see my own face, that's all.'

'Turn it over and… Oh, never mind.' Harriet shook her head and put her visor down before clinging on to Jake. He checked on her once more and then started the motorbike up. He drove very slowly down the drive, turned, and then drove just as slowly back up. Then he did the same thing twice more. Harriet raised her fist occasionally. 'Go faster, go faster!'

Sylvia joyfully wielded Harriet's stick like a lightsaber as Jake's motorbike roared up and down the long driveway, before putting it down to try to take photos with the mobile phone. Jake stopped the motorbike back at the entrance to the Lodge and made as if to get off. Harriet tapped his shoulder and waved him on. Three more times Jake drove up and down the drive, getting steadily faster with each lap. The fourth time, he disappeared with a roar out of the end of the drive and reappeared five minutes later, Harriet waving from the back.

As Jake helped an ecstatic Harriet off the motorbike and steadied her on her feet, Sylvia wheeled over to him and put her hand on his arm. 'Don't look now, but there's a face at the windae that would turn the milk sour.'

'Granda?'

'Aye, son. He's been there all the time we've been out here.' She sneaked a sideways peek at Gregor Abercrombie, who was at his kitchen window. 'He's just standing pretending to do the washing up and making out as though he's not watching.'

'He spoken to you, yet?'

'Naw. He's only been here a year, though. Give him time.' Her sarcastic tone masked a deep hurt.

Jake looked at her solemnly. 'Shall I wave?'

Sylvia shrugged. 'I guess it can't do any harm.'

Jake turned and waved at Gregor, who immediately disappeared without giving any signal that he'd seen his grandson. Jake turned to Sylvia and shrugged. She sighed and Harriet patted her on the back. Although Harriet was now back to being a wizened elderly woman, leaning on her stick in pain, her face was flushed and her eyes were bright. 'You okay, Sylv?'

Sylvia's smile was forced but heartfelt. 'Aye, doll. You enjoy your stint as a biker chick?'

'Magic.' Harriet was about to say something else but a white van appeared, the logo 'Ripping Yarns' on the side, spelled out in an image of wool. A woman hopped nimbly out of the cab.

Sylvia waved at her and explained to Jake, 'Nettie and Erskine's lassie.' She turned back to the woman. 'Alright, Sally? That you bringing Nettie some more of that lovely blue wool?' She made a face at Jake, turning to whisper, 'I sodding hope not. Nettie's flat's full of the stuff. Christ knows what she's going to do with it. The hospital sent back the last lot of baby blankets she knitted. I think they were worried her shite knitting would upset the babies.'

Sally came over for a hug from both Sylvia and Harriet, shaking hands with Jake. 'Aye, Sylvia, just another couple of boxes to keep her going.' She took three large boxes out of the back of the van. 'I know Mum likes this one. They've discontinued this colour, you know.'

'Have they, hen? What a shame. Nettie'll be fair upset.' Sylvia raised an eyebrow at Jake and Harriet behind Sally's back.

'Oh, don't worry; I managed to get hold of some of the old stock. Mum won't run out any time soon. I've another forty boxes in the garage.'

6

Lydia looked up from the untidy and precarious mountain of paperwork on her desk, and tried to hide the look of displeasure as she saw Fergus Lamont through the big window that was all that separated her office from the hallway. She had never liked the man. He seldom took the time to visit his parents; on the rare occasions he did come, it was usually to say that he was putting the rents up, or that the radiators in the corridor should be turned off, or some other money-saving nonsense that took no account of people's lives. She wondered what annoyance he was bringing to her today. He was ushering in a man she'd never seen before. She shivered a little as she caught a glimpse of the scar that cut across one side of the man's face. Lydia had the distinct impression that she'd be happier if she never saw him again.

As she opened the door to her office to greet the two men, she heard Lamont's voice. 'I'll give her the letter and then take you for a tour.' The other man nodded nodded and stopped to read a notice board covered with posters announcing a roast dinner in the function suite, a bingo night, somebody's birthday, and the services of a plethora of mobile chiropodists and hairdressers. Lydia noted that he seemed particularly interested in a printout offering a vibrating pink easy chair for sale.

'Mr Lamont! This is a surprise. We weren't expecting you. Have you come to see your parents? They *will* be pleased; it's been a wee while since you've been in.' She couldn't help the accusatory note that crept into her voice. Lamont's visits to Ailsa and Thomas were few and far between, and when he did come, it was as if he couldn't wait to get away again. She knew that it upset his parents.

'Good morning, Ms Wheelan. No, no. Just… passing by and thought I'd… ah… drop off this letter.' He handed her an envelope. She took it as though it was going to go off in her hand.

The stranger approached Lydia and held out his hand. 'Lovely place you have here, Miss Wheelan. Fergus has told me so much about it.'

She took the outstretched hand reluctantly, ignoring the seemingly purposeful 'Miss', feeling that the least interaction she had with the man, the better, and looked from him to Lamont, whose face was strained and slightly damp with sweat. 'This is… errrr… a friend of mine. Mr Mahoney. He's… errrrr…'

Mahoney broke in, smoothly, all unctuous oiliness. 'Yes, I just happened to mention to Fergus that my parents are getting on a bit, and he told me about the lovely old people's home you run here.'

Lydia's shoulders stiffened. 'Janus Lodge is a retirement community. It's not an old people's home, Mr Mahoney. Everyone lives here independently, in their own flats.'

'Aye. Quite, quite. Old people's retirement community.' He grimaced in what Lydia assumed to be an approximation of a pleasant smile, as though he wasn't used to it. If anything, it made his face look even more sinister than it already was.

Lydia's voice was now icy. 'I do hope Mr Lamont explained to you that this is a very popular place. We do have a long waiting list, I'm afraid.'

Lamont laughed, awkwardly, the sweat on his face now settling darkly onto the collar of his shirt. 'Ms Wheelan, I'm sure that for someone of Gri… errrr… Mr Mahoney's stature we would try and accommodate him and his dear parents.'

Lydia drew herself up and opened her mouth, but before she could speak Mahoney broke in. 'Now, now, Fergus. I'm sure we wouldn't ask for anything unethical, would we. Besides… we have other plans, I believe.' He fixed Lamont with a sharp look that to Lydia looked like some sort of warning. Her unease at the man's presence grew. She would certainly make sure that any application on behalf of his parents was conveniently filed in the bin.

Lamont's head bobbed. 'Aye… errrr… right.' The two men moved off down the hallway and Lydia watched after them for a while, frowning, before eventually going back into her office.

Lamont and Mahoney continued up the corridor in silence. As they did, they passed a door marked 'Toilet'. From inside came the unmistakeable grunts and groans and orgasmic yelps of a couple having noisy sex. Lamont, horror dawning on his face, tried to hurry his companion past the door, but Mahoney stopped dead, fascinated by the noises. Even after the sounds stopped, Mahoney was reluctant to leave the spot, despite Lamont's desperate attempts to interest him in a fire hydrant much further along the corridor.

The door burst open and an elderly couple emerged, looking flushed. The woman was patting ineffectually at her hair, which was a riot of grey curls, and the man was red-faced and beaming, doing up his fly. When they saw the two men they started to smile. The woman spread out her arms as though waiting for Lamont and Mahoney to come and get a hug.

Mahoney was fixed to the spot, delighted by the scene in front of him, but Lamont, flustered, backed away and muttered under his breath, 'Oh, that's all I need.'

The woman tottered after him. 'Fergus! How lovely to see you!'

Lamont brushed her off, as if she were an annoying fly. 'Yes, yes. Whatever. I can't stop now.' He pushed his way past the pair of them, studiously ignoring the woman's welcoming arms.

Her face fell. 'But Fergus, it's been ages since you've been to see us. We love it when you visit, you know that.'

Mahoney nodded politely and moved past the now clearly distraught woman. He set off in Lamont's wake, throwing a final, half-calculating, half-appreciative look back at the elderly couple. Lamont sped up, without a backwards glance.

The woman slowly lowered her arms and called after them, plaintively, 'Fergus?'

The man with her took her gently by the arm and turned her to face him. 'Wee arsehole. Forget it, hen. He's just a wee arsehole.'

*

'Ohgodohgodohgodohgod.' Lydia opened a drawer and took out a bottle of painkillers, deftly opened the lid one-handed, still with her eyes on the letter in her other hand, and popped a couple of the tablets dry, swallowing them with a grimace. 'This cannot be happening.' She pressed a thumb and forefinger tightly against the top of her nose and then went out into the hallway. She could see Lamont and his friend at the end of the corridor, coming back down the wide staircase that led up to the rest of the flats and the cinema and library. Their visit had been brief, but not brief enough for her liking. She waited outside her office, shaking with anger. 'I'd like a word, please, Mr Lamont.'

The two men looked at each other and stepped towards her door, but Lydia stepped in front of them and held up a hand to stop Mahoney from accompanying him, her usual politeness put aside. 'Alone, if you wouldn't mind.'

Mahoney stepped back with that hideous smile again. 'Of course, Miss Wheelan.' There it was again, the patronising 'Miss'.

'It's Ms. Ms Wheelan.'

Mahoney simply bowed his head, his mouth twitching briefly. 'Fergus, I'll wait for you in the car.'

Lamont squeaked out a response and followed Lydia into her office. She shut the door, watching until Mahoney had exited the building. She turned and waved the letter at Lamont. 'What's all this about?'

Lamont crossed his arms and surveyed his shoes as though he'd never seen them before. 'Ah… well… you see…'

The letter rustled furiously as Lydia waved it at him. 'You want to sell this building?'

He looked up and smiled at her in an ingratiating way. 'Yes… that is…'

Lydia held up her hand. 'More precisely, you want to turn our residents out of their homes to turn this place into some sort of club?'

Lamont put his head down again, vaguely sheepish. 'Well… yes. That's about the strength of it, yes.'

Lydia put a hand on her desk to steady herself. She took a deep breath. 'But, as I'm sure you'll agree, Janus Lodge is a very lucrative business with an excellent reputation. We run a tight ship here, Mr Lamont, as you know. We've got a waiting list as long as your arm. Elderly people are fighting each other to get in… not literally, of course, but…' Lydia rubbed her temples. The pain and nervous tension were making her babble. 'This is *home* for our residents. Some of them have been here for over twenty years – since your grandfather founded the place, in fact.' Surely that appeal to family would make him see sense. 'For many of them, upping walking sticks and moving somewhere else would cause terrible trauma. Surely you can't mean this?'

Lamont would not look her in the eyes. 'Mr Mahoney has made an excellent offer and…'

Mahoney. So that's why he was here with Lamont. Lydia felt the bile rise in her throat. He was the one behind this sale. And, of course, it was all about money; that was all Lamont cared about. But he seemed to have forgotten one thing. 'Besides, as you are well aware, under the terms of your grandfather's will, the residents have first refusal to buy the property in the event of a sale and have to be given all reasonable time and opportunity to do so.'

Lamont shook his head. 'No. I hadn't forgotten it, Ms Wheelan.'

'How much has this man Mahoney offered?'

Lamont cleared his throat. 'Three… and a half… million was the amount suggested.'

Three and a half million? Where would they ever find that amount of money? Lydia felt as though her knees would give way, but she steadied herself. 'You do realise, Mr Lamont, that, according to the legal papers that your grandfather drew up, your parents are to be looked after here until their deaths. And, as I am sure you realised when you saw them in the hallway just now, they are both in rude health. *Very* rude health.' She had him now, she was sure.

Lamont blushed and cleared his throat, but seemed on firmer ground when he spoke again. 'Ah, well, no, you see, Ms Wheelan, the clause doesn't say they have to be looked after *here*. It just says that they have to be looked after.' He beamed at her. 'With three and a half million pounds, I can get them a wee flat, somewhere quiet, with someone to look after them twenty-four hours a day.' Lydia got the impression that he was thinking of somewhere very small, very quiet, and, most importantly, very far away from him.

There was a knock at the door and Mahoney poked his head in. 'Sorry to interrupt this little *tête-à-tête*, but I need to get back to the office. My businesses don't run themselves, you know.' Lydia shuddered; in his mouth, the phrase *tête-à-tête* sounded sinister and creepy.

Lamont stood. 'Of course, Gri— Mahoney.' He walked out of the office without another word to Lydia, leaving her office door wide open. She watched the two men as they walked out, Mahoney with a proprietary hand on Lamont's shoulder, steering him towards a silver Mercedes that stood in the drive. The car was flanked by two hideous-looking men in tracksuits, who stood to attention like two trained monkeys when they saw Mahoney.

Lamont and Mahoney stood for a moment and looked back at the façade of the building. Lydia drew her cardigan around herself more closely, feeling a sudden chill that wasn't just the autumn air, and went back into her office and closed the blinds.

'She's not happy, as I'm sure you could hear on the other side of that door. She picked up on that clause in the contract and could make things very difficult for us. So, we don't want her getting hold of the fact that you want to build a… gentlemen's club.'

Grinder removed a non-existent thread from his mohair coat and turned up his collar. 'Think they'll be able to raise the cash?'

Lamont scoffed. 'A bunch of old biddies like that? Not a chance. Oh, by the way, the price has gone up. It's three and a half million now.' The idea had come to him in Lydia Wheelan's office, so why not make it official?

Grinder raised an eyebrow. 'Three and a half? And how do you work that out?' His voice was as cold as the air.

Lamont shrugged. 'I need to protect myself a wee bit. This sort of deal could break me if it goes tits up, you know. It's just… a wee bit more delicate selling to you than it is selling to anyone else.' He gestured with his head towards Janus Lodge. 'These are a bunch of nice old duffers who want to keep their home. You, on the other hand...' He let the sentence drift off. It probably wasn't wise to continue.

But Grinder clearly wasn't going to let that one lie. 'I, on the other hand?'

Lamont coloured. 'Aye, well, you're going to throw out a bunch of pensioners to knock it down to build a brothel. That's never going to be popular. Besides, look at this place.' He gestured towards the solid and well-maintained sandstone façade of Janus Lodge, glowing in the late October sun. 'I still don't know how you think you're going to get that one past the council.'

Grinder inspected his beautifully shaped and buffed nails. 'First of all, it's not a brothel, Fergus; it's a gentlemen's club. Secondly, I have a connection on the council who... well... let's just say he owes me a favour.' He moved closer to Lamont, his face looming towards him. PJ and Declan, ever vigilant, took a step forward. 'And finally, I don't know what you take me for, but I'm a businessman. And.' He poked an accusing finger in Lamont's chest. 'Businessman to businessman, we have a deal. I do hope you haven't forgotten that?'

Lamont blinked rapidly and swallowed a few times. 'No need to get mad, Grinder. We've still got a deal; it's just... changed a wee bit, is all. It's *my* reputation that's on the line here, and I need a wee bit of an insurance policy.' The flammable shell suits rustled as PJ and Declan took another step closer. Lamont eased a finger under his collar, nervously. 'Call off the dogs, Grinder, eh? We'll talk about it, right? I'm sure we'll come to some sort of compromise.'

Mahoney signalled to his heavies and walked towards the car. 'Well, compromise is not a word that happens to be in my thesaurus, Fergus. Lads, it looks as though we won't have time to take Mr Lamont back to his office after all.' PJ and Declan scrambled to open the driver's door for Mahoney and then clambered into the car themselves. The Mercedes eased its smooth, efficient way down the drive, leaving Lamont staring at them in shock.

He called after them. 'But... but how am I supposed to get back?'

A window opened on PJ's side and a casual flick of the vickies was raised in response.

7

THE HALLWAY OF JANUS LODGE WAS EMPTY. The hallways were *always* empty once residents had tucked themselves up for the evening. Keys turned simultaneously in locks as the theme tune for the BBC *News at Six* rang out on TVs all over the building. It was as though the regular siren call of the news reminded the residents that there was a wide world out there beyond their calm and peaceful environment that was grimy and unpleasant and often dangerous. The office was shut and locked for the day, but the residents were secure in the knowledge that, if needed, Lydia Wheelan was only a phone call or the pull of a red alarm string away.

A man in a black puffer jacket and a woollen hat pulled down over his ears let himself in through the front door carrying a bundle of brown envelopes. The automatic locking system didn't take effect until nine at night in the summer and seven in the winter. The man walked up the hallway, inserting an envelope into each of the letter boxes as he passed, starting with the one nearest the doors and criss-crossing to each of the doors in turn. He whistled tunelessly, obviously a man who was happy in his work. As he reached the end of the corridor, one of the doors he'd already posted his missive through slammed, and he turned as he heard a wheelchair being wheeled up the corridor towards him at high speed.

'Haw! Haw, you… Whistling Willy. What the fuck is this?'

The man turned around. Sylvia, positively apoplectic, waved the letter he had just put through her door.

He scratched his head, confused. 'Eh… it's a letter, hen.'

Sylvia brandished the letter closer towards him. 'Aye, I know it's a letter, ya wee wank. What I mean is, what's it all about?'

He took the letter from her and started to read it, rather laboriously. '*Dear Resident, this is to give you six months to quit Janus Lodge due to redev—*'

'Fucksake, daftarse, I know *what* it says; I want to know *why*.'

The man shrugged and handed the letter back to her. 'Beats me, hen. The boss just asked me to deliver them; I didnae write them.' He turned and posted an envelope through the last door in the hallway, then turned to walk up the stairs to deliver the rest of the letters.

Sylvia wheeled her chair to the bottom of the staircase, unable to follow him any further. She called up after him. 'Next time, tell your boss to do his own dirty work. Send the organ grinder, not his monkey. I'd like a word wi' him, whoever he is.'

8

All of Janus Lodge's residents were gathered in the communal lounge, along with Lydia Wheelan, the kitchen staff, cleaning staff and the woman who did the handywork around the building. The mood was unusually subdued, and a few people were clearly holding back tears. Nettie Forbes was crying on her husband Erskine's shoulder. Lydia Wheelan had just finished explaining the situation to them all. 'And I'm so sorry you had to find out in that way, that should never have happened. I'll be speaking to them about that.'

Francine raised her hand and Lydia nodded at her. 'And you say there's absolutely nothing we can do to stop them?'

Lydia shrugged. 'I've put the question to our lawyers to look into the deed that determines what can and can't be done, but failing that, no, not unless we can raise three and a half million pounds.'

Sylvia wheeled herself forward. 'Well? Why can't we?'

Gregor Abercrombie snorted. 'And how the hell do you think we're going to do that, you stupid woman? We're pensioners, not millionaires. Besides, we're all at least seventy. What can *we* do?'

Loretta Niven, a slim, stylish woman with dyed blonde hair sprayed to within an inch of its life, raised a carefully manicured hand and they all turned to look at her. 'Actually, I'm sixty-seven.'

Gregor looked her up and down. 'Aye, mibbee a decade ago, before you started going senile.'

A dapper elderly gent standing next to Loretta stepped forward. He was tall and of military bearing, with a neat moustache. 'I say, Gregor.

I think you should apologise to the lady.' Abercrombie snorted and squared up to Loretta's knight errant. The two glared at each other and puffed out their chests like wheezy pigeons.

Lydia stepped in between them and Loretta grabbed the man by the hand. 'Thank you, Archie… for defending my honour.' She lowered her eyelashes coyly. Archie twirled his moustache as if he was Clark Gable in *Gone with the Wind* and bowed slightly over Loretta's hand, giving it a lingering kiss.

As Gregor retched theatrically in response, Lydia broke in. 'Look, I know this is really upsetting for everyone. But you can rest assured that I'm going to do everything I can to see that this doesn't happen.' She looked around the room at the unhappy and hopeless faces in front of her and her voice broke slightly. 'Please, please, please – I want you all to try not to worry about it. We've got six months to try to raise the money and he can't even *start* the process in the meantime. This place won't be sold from under us, don't worry.' Several of the residents shook their heads. 'Don't give up. There's lots we can do.'

Gregor Abercrombie snorted. 'Like what?'

'Well, for a start, I'm going to contact our MP, go to the council, see if we can get some money from the Lottery Fund…' Lydia trailed off, distraught.

Harriet Knox stepped gingerly forward. She leaned heavily on her stick, but waved Lydia away when she moved to help her. 'I've looked up yer man Fergus Lamont on Google and checked out his company on the Companies House database. He seems to be a wee bit of a ruthless bastard, from all the evidence.' She held up a sheaf of paper. 'This isn't the first time he's done something like this. Actually, it seems that it's a bit out of character for him to give us six months' notice. He usually snaps property up and turns it around for a healthy profit without seeming to care whose lives he's destroying in the process. He threw out the residents of a homeless hostel earlier this year with only two weeks' notice.'

A rumble of sighs and sobs went around the room. Thomas and Ailsa Lamont, who had been sitting quietly at the back, looked at each other and stood up. Ailsa cleared her throat. 'I think that might be because of us.' Everyone looked around at them. 'I'm afraid that ruthless bastard is our son. You may not have realised that because he… he doesn't visit very often.'

Thomas grabbed onto her hand. 'My father, Fergus's grandfather, didn't like him and had a clause written into his will to say that Ailsa and I must be cared for, for the rest of our lives. I'm afraid that the reason he's giving us as much as six months is so he won't have to have us go and live with him in his enormous house while he finds us somewhere else. And he definitely doesn't want that. Says we embarrass him.'

Ailsa leaned forward and whispered loudly, 'He says we spend too much time having sex.' She looked at Thomas and opened her eyes wide. 'As if that was even possible.'

9

ALL THE BINGO NIGHT NOTICES, LINE-DANCE POSTERS and invitations to Francine's martial arts classes had been removed from the notice board at Janus Lodge. Now, it was covered in rousing rhetoric: a handwritten notice inviting all the residents to an Extraordinary General Meeting, all in bold capital letters: 'WE SHALL NOT BE MOVED, BROTHERS AND SISTERS. WE SHALL OVERCOME'; exhortations to fellow residents to stand firm; requests for ideas to raise money; calls to arms to resist the capitalist oppressor; and reminders that the wartime spirit was not dead.

Everyone was crammed into one of Janus Lodge's meeting rooms for the EGM. Extra chairs had been brought in to accommodate all those who wanted to be there. Nervous chatter was bubbling as the amassed residents waited for the meeting to be called to attention. Erskine and Archie were discussing the relative levels of their blood pressure and the merits of walnuts for lowering cholesterol.

Archie sighed. 'Bloody tablets, eh? I take sixteen of them every bloody day. And that's not to mention all the supplements. Calcium, cod liver oil, Vitamin D…'

Erskine nodded sagely. 'B12, probiotics, folic acid…'

'Vitamin E, Vitamin C, Ashwaganda—'

Before they could continue the litany of magical lotions and potions, Francine banged a gavel on the table and all noise ceased. 'Order, ladies and gentlemen. This meeting will come to order if you please.' Everyone looked at her attentively. 'Now, as this is an Extraordinary Meeting we will move straight to our only order of business – the future of Janus Lodge. Can I take comments from the floor, please?' One of the elderly men raised his hand and Francine nodded. 'The Chair recognises Mr McKee.'

McKee stood and cleared his throat. 'Madam President, I'd like to propose that the front door be locked at six o'clock during the winter months, rather than seven o'clock as at present.'

Francine shook her head. 'I'm afraid that's normal committee business and therefore it's *ultra vires* for the purposes of this meeting, Mr McKee. Please raise it at the next regular committee meeting and we'll take it under consideration then.' McKee sat down again, mumbling. Francine looked around the room. 'Next?' McKee put his hand up once again. 'The Chair recognises Mr McKee.'

Mr McKee stood up once more. 'Madam Chairman, I've mentioned before that the lights in the hallways should remain on all night. Andrew Snelling in number 22 keeps turning them off. But it's against health and safety to have them switched off. Any of us could come out and break our necks.'

Francine nodded. 'A well-made point, as ever, Mr McKee.' Mr McKee preened and sat back down, waiting expectantly for the admonishment of Andrew Snelling, who was sitting glowering in a corner of the overcrowded room. 'However, if we could keep *regular* business for the next *regular* meeting and concentrate on the matter in hand, I would be grateful. Now, does anyone else have any points to raise?' McKee raised his hand and Francine sighed. Rumbles of annoyance went around the room. Francine's voice was sharp. 'The Chair recognises Mr McKee.'

McKee stood with some difficulty for a third time. 'Madam Chairman-Person, Mr Walsh in number 32 has been riding his mobility scooter drunk, yet again. I'd like to propose that he be banned from riding it through the hallway for six months and made to attend some sort of addiction counselling. The man's a liability.'

'Oh for fu—'

'Sylvia!' Francine slapped Sylvia on the arm and impatiently waved Mr McKee back into his seat. 'Again, that's *ultra vires* and should be raised at the next regular meeting, Mr McKee.'

Francine's tone was designed to silence McKee, but he ploughed on, single-mindedly and unadvisedly. 'But the man's dangerous.'

'I think we're all aware of that, Mr McKee, but could we please shelve that motion until the next regular meeting?' McKee opened his mouth to speak again but Francine continued before he had the chance. 'Now, does anyone have any comments on the purpose of this meeting? To be *quite* clear, that's the proposed sale of Janus Lodge.'

Mr McKee raised his hand, and Sylvia slapped a hand on the table and said, more loudly this time, 'Oh for fu—'

Francine banged her gavel. 'Sylvia!'

'Sorry, Madam Dominatrix… errrr… Madam Chairman, sir.'

Francine raised her eyebrows and Harriet prodded Sylvia in the ribs. Francine looked sternly around the room. 'Now, as I have said, several times now, does anyone have any comments or suggestions related to today's order of business? Namely – how we are going to raise the three and a half million pounds which we need in order to save Janus Lodge from the developers.'

Mr McKee finally put his hand down.

10

The communal lounge was, as usual, full of the sounds of knitting needles clacking and the chink of fancy china cups being placed on matching saucers. Francine was finishing off her expertly made sweater, Nettie was painstakingly frowning over yet another disturbingly misshapen baby blanket. Sylvia – her usual Guinness can to hand – was crocheting intricate flowers, a pile of which lay on the table beside her. Loretta was knitting Archie a green and gold Celtic scarf, while he was holding the skein for her lovingly. Over in the corner, several more elderly women were feverishly knitting.

Instead of the usual companionable chit-chat, however, there was a palpable sense of tension over the room and a few whispered conversations in worried voices about trying to find somewhere else to live. Unusually, Harriet was sitting at the next table to Sylvia, with a laptop in front of her and a large accounts book to one side. She wasn't a knitter and was seldom seen outside of her flat – or 'Mission Control', as Sylvia called it. It was often difficult to prise her away from her computer screens. Sylvia watched her fingers whizz over the keyboard. 'You're the Ayrton Senna of the keyboard, doll. What's the total to date?'

Harriet leaned back and sighed. 'Well, we made £167 from the bake sale on Saturday, plus a couple of hundred from the computer parts I sold on eBay. Francine's new children's Judo class at the community centre brought in just over £50, which I think we can expect every week. Then there was the used book sale, so our current total is £4,825.' She sighed again. 'The problem is, we're mostly just selling stuff to each other. And, unfortunately, all of us put together don't have even a tenth of what we need to buy this place.'

Sylvia crushed the Guinness can in her hand as if she wished it were Fergus Lamont's head. 'Bugger me, that's utter shite. We've been at this for three weeks and that's all we've made? We're never going to get anywhere near that three and a half million at this rate. Should have taken up my suggestion in the first place.'

Harriet absent-mindedly picked up the crushed can and threw it, without looking, into the wastepaper basket in the corner of the room. It landed in the centre of the bin without even touching the sides. She smiled and Sylvia nodded at her appreciatively.

Nettie frowned over another dropped stitch. 'I don't think that would be a good idea, Sylvia, dear. I don't think even you could make a swift and unobtrusive getaway from a bank robbery in that wheelchair. And the rest of us don't stand an earthly.'

Harriet stood up with some difficulty and tottered over to the window, leaning heavily on her stick. Outside, several plants marked 'FOR SALE' sat forlornly on the frosty wooden decking. 'Sylv's right, though. We're going to have to do something drastic. We need some serious 360-degree thinking here. It's no good relying on bake sales here and a few dejected plants there. We need something that's scalable.' Sylvia, Nettie and Francine all paused as one in their knitting and stared at Harriet. 'We need to do some blue sky thinking and brainstorm a list of quick wins. Something that will give us traction in the marketplace.'

The other three looked at each other. Francine raised her eyebrows and Sylvia made a circular movement at her forehead with one of her knitting needles. Nettie let her knitting fall to the floor and raised her hands to her face, ignoring the blanket as it unravelled. 'But what can we *do*?'

Harriet eased herself gently back into her chair, wincing as her knees cracked. 'There must be something we can do that has the potential to raise substantial funds. We need to upskill.'

'Upskill? We're too old to upskill.' Nettie's voice wavered. 'Are you saying we should all go out and get jobs?'

But Sylvia started to applaud. Everyone in the room stopped what they were doing and looked at her. 'Well said, Harriet, doll. We mustn't take this lying down. We've got to think of something. We may be old, but we're not dead yet. That bastard Lamont is underestimating us if he thinks we're just going to lie down and take it up the arse like a jailhouse punk.'

Francine gave her a stern look and opened her mouth to say something, then simply sighed and shook her head.

Harriet tapped at her laptop once more. 'Sylvia's correct. We need to leverage our talents more. We need a take-to-market strategy and some forward thinking.' She looked around at them all. 'I think sometimes people look at us and only see elderly people. They forget we were lawyers, doctors, teachers, artists, entrepreneurs.'

Sylvia nodded slowly. 'Sometimes *we* forget it.'

A silence descended on the room; it was clear that Sylvia's words had hit home. Then the clacking of needles resumed again as the knitters bent their heads in concentration. Harriet gazed off into the distance for a moment and then brought her focus back to the room. She looked around at the industrious knitters, then her eyes flitted over some of the many, many results of this industriousness that bedecked the room in glorious Technicolor. 'Oh my God. It's staring us in the face.' She stood again, this time ignoring the pain from her joints, and walked around the room, her stick tapping on the variety of knitted items as she passed. 'Look at it all. Look at all this talent; people are crying out for stuff like this.' She finished her tour around the room. 'Nettie – how much of that free baby-blue wool can you get hold of, exactly? You know, with a concerted effort and a judicious marketing strategy, we can be best of breed.'

Nettie, puzzled, turned to Francine and Sylvia. 'Best of breed? Did she just call me a cow?'

11

Fergus Lamont reached into his desk drawer for the bottle of antacids he kept there. On the other end of the phone, the monotonous voice kept up its droning, repeating itself for the third time. Fergus cut the woman off. 'Look, I've told you already; this letter you've sent me is outrageous. The sale can't be delayed any further. I already have to wait six months before I can even *think* of putting it on the market. Why do I have to wait even longer?'

The woman on the other end of the phone sighed. 'I've already told you, Mr Lamont.' She repeated herself for the fourth time, as if to an extremely dim two-year-old. 'We've received correspondence from the lawyers of a Ms Lydia Wheelan, on behalf of the residents of Janus Lodge—'

'Yes, yes. I know all that. But they *can't* delay it any longer. They just can't.'

The sigh came once more, this time louder and longer. 'But that's the whole point. They *can*, Mr Lamont. Under the terms of your grandfather's will, your parents have the right to live at Janus Lodge for the rest of their natural lives.'

'But I can find them somewhere else to live, that's what his will says, doesn't it?'

The woman hesitated and Fergus's stomach churned as if on cue. 'Not… exactly. Your parents can live with you, yes.'

Lamont chugged down another antacid. 'What? But I don't *want* them living with me.'

The silence on the other end of the phone was a disapproving one. 'Then you don't have a choice. They either live with you, or they stay at Janus Lodge while they are both still alive. The terms are clear.'

Lamont spied a tiny ray of light. 'So, they *both* have to be alive?' The disapproving silence stretched out and he realised what she must be thinking. 'I mean… my father isn't in the best of health.' Although what he had seen at Janus Lodge and would never be able to wipe from his mind even with therapy would seem to disprove that.

Finally, the lawyer spoke. 'No. Should your father predecease your mother then she is to remain at Janus Lodge until her own death. And vice versa, of course.' Her tone was frosty, to say the least.

There were no more antacids left in the bottle. 'What if I were to build them a house on the grounds of my property?' A very small house. With a big fence. Plenty of soundproofing. His wife wouldn't be happy, but he needed this sale. Things hadn't been looking good recently.

The woman hesitated for a moment. 'Well, possibly. I'd need to check the will and associated contract once again. But… well… that's the other thing, Mr Lamont. I'm afraid that we aren't going to be able to act on your behalf any longer.'

A lump formed in Lamont's chest. The antacids weren't doing their job. 'What do you mean?'

'Just what I said. I'm afraid that your values no longer align with those of this firm. You need to find another lawyer. And very soon.'

His values had *never* aligned with theirs. She must know that. His eyes flicked over to the crumpled newspaper in his wastepaper basket. 'You've seen *The Herald*, haven't you?'

Her voice was sharp. 'Of course. And the *Evening Times*, *The Scotsman* and *The National*. "Property mogul evicts OAPs, including own parents" isn't the sort of headline we at this firm want to be associated with.'

Bitch. 'You've been happy to accept my money all these years, and for all that time you've known what my business involves. And, more to the point, who. And you must be aware that certain parties will be very unhappy at this development.'

She paused a moment, and when she spoke her voice was even colder than previously. 'Is that a threat, Mr Lamont?'

'Not at all.'

'Good. I'm very pleased to hear that.'

'But I…' Fergus found that he was speaking to dead air. As he threw his mobile across the room, followed by the empty antacid bottle, the phone on his desk rang. 'What?!'

'Now, now, Fergus.' Grinder's silky tones somehow made the pain in his chest even worse. Was he having a heart attack? He rubbed at the spot. Probably just indigestion.

'Sorry, Grinder. Bad day. Look, if you're ringing about Janus Lodge, I'm—'

'Not today. But yes, it would be good if you could get your act together on that one. Have you seen the papers? The publicity isn't exactly stellar, although I was pleased to see that my name wasn't mentioned. You haven't told anyone my plans, have you?'

Lamont rubbed at the bridge of his nose. He was getting a headache now. 'Of course not, but that Wheelan woman has already told the press that you're involved, and you can't blame me for that. That annoying *Herald* journalist has been back on to me again today, looking for a quote. We shouldn't have gone out there together; that was foolish.'

'Ah, well, no matter. Give me the name; journalists can always be bought off. And we can see about shutting the Wheelan woman up at some point.' Lamont closed his eyes and shuddered at how this might happen. 'No, I'm calling about the bookies in Springfield Road. The one nearest to Janus Lodge, coincidentally.'

Lamont was puzzled. 'What about it?' Things were running smoothly there – a bit quiet at the moment, but that would pick up. Gambling was something which would never go out of fashion. On the other end of the phone, he could hear the umistakeable sound of Grinder filing his nails.

'Profits are down. You'll need to let someone go.'

'Let someone go? But there's only Agnes and that gormless young twat you made me employ. There's not even a cleaner; Agnes does it all.'

'Mmmmm, yes. That gormless young twat, as you call him – correctly, as it happens – is Aidan, my sister's boy. He has to stay, unfortunately. What about the security guard?'

'But that would leave us exposed. We're already at a disadvantage just having the one. All your other bookies have two.'

Mahoney's voice was exasperated. 'Look, Fergus, I shouldn't need to tell you your job. Profits are down, cuts need to be made, somebody has to go. And I assume you don't want it to be you. So sort it.'

For the second time that morning, Fergus was left staring at a silent phone.

12

The communal lounge was a hive of sharply focused activity. Nettie, Francine and Sylvia were in their usual places. Every other seat contained a resident knitting furiously. Everyone had been called into service. Loretta was teaching Archie and Nettie's husband Erskine to loom knit, and they were turning out tiny bobble hats for babies at an impressive speed. Harriet was hobbling around with an iPad in one hand and her stick in the other, directing operations and pausing occasionally to enter some data onto the tablet.

A big table had been set up at one end of the room. It was currently covered in neat piles of completed items awaiting packing – blankets, shawls, scarves, hats, gloves, cardigans… and a pathetic little pile of badly made baby blankets in pale blue. In fact, there was a preponderance of baby blue amongst the items laid out. There was also an A4 notepad on the table. Harriet moved over to the table and started checking items off in the notepad, her eyes flicking from notepad to iPad, her regular round of stocktaking. She beckoned over two elderly men who were sitting waiting patiently for that very summons. They started to pack and label the items on the table, and deposit them in a row of open boxes that were laid out next to the closed patio doors.

Harriet was humming happily to herself, clearly completely in her element. Every now and again, she tore a page out of the A4 pad, screwed it into a ball, and expertly threw it into a wastepaper basket in the corner of the room. Now a normal underarm throw, the next time overarm, then backwards, over her head and finally through her legs. This one took her a few moments to stretch back up from, but each time the ball of paper slammed squarely into the middle of the basket. Everyone else in the room completely ignored her; initially, they had marvelled at her throwing skills, the result of her baseball career in America, but now they were used to it.

Sylvia's grandson, Jake, as usual clad all in leather and still wearing his motorcycle helmet, entered the room. He was carrying a leather sports bag. He waved a hand to everyone and went over to give his grandmother a kiss. As she raised her face to him, he took off his helmet; underneath, he was wearing a neat balaclava in baby blue. Knitted into the back of the balaclava, in bright red wool, was an expertly designed skull and crossbones. He removed the balaclava and put it into his pocket, kissing Sylvia as he did so. She looked optimistically at him, and he reached into his bag and pulled out a four-pack of Guinness, which he put down on the table next to her. 'Alright, Gran?' He smiled over at Francine and Nettie. 'A few more of the boys want one of the special balaclavas, can you do me another eight, Francine?'

'Of course. Happy to.' She nodded over towards Harriet, who was frowning as she tapped away at her iPad. 'Go and give your order to the boss, would you. She rules us with an iron… whatever that gizmo is she's got there.'

Sylvia tutted. 'It's a peapod, Francine. Get with the techy trend, will you.'

Jake rumbled out a laugh. 'Jeez, Gran. When did you suddenly become such an expert on technology?'

Sylvia slapped out at him. 'Ya cheeky wee shite. The World Wide Web is not just the purview of the younger generation, you know, despite what you think.'

Jake looked at Francine and mouthed, *Purview?* Francine simply shook her head and raised her eyebrows.

Sylvia ignored them both, pointedly, before continuing airily. 'In fact, Harriet's teaching me how to use the internet more effectively, so I can help her run the business.'

Jake's mouth dropped open. 'Teaching you to…?'

Sylvia waved a hand, expansively. 'Insta, Facebook, Tickety-Tockety, Sunny Skies… It's going to be my job to interact with our younger demographic… you know, get down with the kids… and… stuff.'

Jake groaned. 'Oh, shite.'

Sylvia smiled happily. 'Aye, we're gonnae make some wee films and download them up. Get the virus going. She says millions of people will see them.'

'Shite,' Jake muttered once more.

Francine leaned across and patted his hand. 'Quite, Jake. Quite. Now, don't think about that any more – it will only worry you. God knows, it's been worrying *me* ever since I heard about it. Your grandmother running riot on the internet is not something I want to dwell on. Now, go and see Harriet and give her your order.'

As Jake went over to her, Harriet's mobile phone started to ring. 'Dance of the Knights' by Prokofiev. Jake turned back round to Francine. 'Is that—'

Francine smiled. 'Yes, dear. The theme tune from *The Apprentice*. She changed it last week. She's a big fan of Alan Sugar.'

Harriet answered the phone. She no longer sounded like an elderly woman in pain, as she had only a couple of weeks before. Instead, she sounded like Margaret Thatcher on steroids. 'Hello, Janus Knitwear. CEO speaking… Yes… uh-huh… uh-huh… We can develop a bespoke solution to your needs, for sure. Yup… win-win, uh-huh… Let me touch base with my people and I'll bell you later. K… K… Buhbye, bye, buhbye.' She firmly pressed the off button on the phone and smiled at Jake, holding a finger up as he opened his mouth to speak. She tapped furiously at the iPad and then wrote something in her notebook. 'Loretta – that's two hundred more chicken jumpers.' Loretta waved at her, happily.

Jake was puzzled. 'Chicken jumpers?'

'Yes, Jakey. For bald chickens.' From her tone of voice, anyone would think that was the most normal statement in the world, and Jake wasn't sure what to say, so simply relayed his balaclava order.

As Harriet tapped the order into her iPad, her phone rang again. 'Janus Knitwear. CEO Harriet Knox speaking.' Jake kissed her on the cheek, said his goodbyes to the rest of them, put his balaclava back on and shrugged into his helmet, giving them all a final wave as he left through the patio doors.

Just after he had gone, Gregor Abercrombie appeared in the doorway of the lounge holding a newspaper. He cast around for somewhere to sit and stood hesitating, looking around almost wistfully. Sylvia looked up. Her face darkened for a moment, then she smiled slightly and waved him over. He looked at her, and the wistful look changed to his usual glare of steely immobility. He shook his head and marched out of the room without a backwards glance.

Nettie caught her eye and shook her head, questioningly. Sylvia shrugged and returned to her knitting, but Nettie put her hands on her hips. 'What's wrong with that man? He's so… unpleasant.'

Francine threw a concerned look at Sylvia, who kept her head down but said lightly, 'Aye, he is that, hen. But… he didn't always used to be.'

Nettie dropped a stitch in surprise. 'Oh! Did you know him before he came here? I know you and Francine have been here for years, but I thought he only came last year.'

Sylvia untied a knot in her wool. 'Aye, he did, Nettie. Just a couple of months before you and Erskine moved in. I don't know who was the most shocked when he turned up, me or him.' She took a big swig of Guinness.

'How did you know him?'

Francine looked at Sylvia, as if checking that she was okay. Sylvia smiled reassuringly at her. 'Well, the surname might give it away. We were married… to each other, I mean, Nettie, love. Got divorced… ooooh… nearly forty years ago. Our daughter died when Jake was just a wee bairn, and it sort of… changed everything. Changed Gregor, anyway. There was no future for us after that.' Her eyes remained determinedly focused on her knitting.

Nettie stared at her amazed, as every single stitch of her baby blanket dropped off her needles. 'But why? Surely a tragedy like that would…'

Francine reached over and touched her arm. 'Not now, Nettie. Not in front of this lot.'

13

Gregor's flat was plain and dark. There were no ornaments, no photographs, no cheery mementos of holidays past. The place looked as though he had planned only for a temporary stay. He sat down heavily on his bed and opened the battered photo album, turning the pages slowly. Photos of himself as a baby in the 1930s with a widely smiling couple; as a small boy on the beach at Blackpool during Glasgow Fair, chasing after a donkey; and as a beaming young man in RAF uniform with his proud parents. He hesitated before turning the next page, but there he was, looking dapper in a teddy boy outfit, with a beautiful girl in a poodle skirt on his arm – Sylvia. They both looked happy and very much in love, and they were. Because Sylvia's legs were both very much still working.

Then their wedding photos, followed by the happy couple with a baby, lots of photos of a little girl as a toddler, as a teenager, and then as a young lady with her beau. Another wedding photo – this time with Gregor and Sylvia as the beaming parents of the bride. That they were still happy and still madly in love shone out of every picture. He turned the page again. A new baby with its ecstatic grandparents: there were pages and pages of those photos. Gregor smiled softly and lingered on one of the photos, his favourite: him holding the tiny bairn high above his head, both of them with mouths open wide in laughter. He sighed and continued turning the pages, the wee mite of a baby growing with each turn, a personal flipbook of his life.

And there it was, the one he'd been dreading: Jake as a wee boy in his mother's arms, wearing a little blue sailor suit and holding out a teddy towards whoever was behind the camera. Gregor remembered the day. He'd been the cameraman on that occasion. He ran a calloused finger gently over his daughter's face. He didn't need to turn the next page. There was nothing there. There'd been no photos since. But he leafed through the empty pages that followed, as if he could conjure up an alternate life in which his daughter was still alive. A life that would mean he didn't have to suffer in this one.

Gregor sat for a moment on the bed, looking at the last page of the album, as blank and empty as the previous few, then closed it slowly. He stood up and walked over to the wardrobe, bending down to tuck the album away right at the bottom, where it belonged, firmly shutting the wardrobe door on his memories. He walked out of the bedroom and into the bathroom.

He hesitated and then opened the bathroom cabinet. On one shelf a toothbrush, denture tablets, razor, shaving foam and brush lay neatly in a row. On another, four bottles of sleeping tablets. Gregor ran a finger across the top of the bottles and then slowly closed the cabinet door, staring for a long moment at his face in the mirror.

14

HARRIET WAS STILL BARKING INSTRUCTIONS INTO HER mobile and tapping the iPad. Everyone else was busily knitting – with the exception of Nettie, who was sitting with a mess of wool on her lap, her mouth still hanging open, staring at the door where Gregor had stood a few minutes before. 'But why did everything change? Was it because of your daughter's death?'

'Nettie, I don't think…'

Sylvia leaned forward. 'It's alright, Francine, doll.' She drew in a breath and squared her shoulders. 'My daughter died in a car accident, Nettie. We were on our way to do some shopping. All I needed was a loaf of bread and a couple of pints of milk. It could have waited.' She looked off into the distance, as if half remembering, half trying to rewrite history.

Nettie waited a few seconds, before prompting her. 'You said "we"?'

Sylvia nodded slowly. 'She insisted on coming with me; she wanted to tell me all about a job she was going to apply for. So I was in the car, too. That's how I ended up…' She gestured to her wheelchair.

Nettie gasped and put a hand to her mouth. 'Oh no! I had no idea. But why did Gregor…?'

Sylvia concentrated on her crocheting so she didn't need to look at Nettie; but her hands were shaking, and she had lost her usual brash and breezy disposition. 'Gregor was…' Her voice broke. Francine put out a hand and laid it gently on her arm. Sylvia rested her own veined hand on Francine's and nodded at her, unable to continue the story herself.

Francine clasped Sylvia's hand tight and turned to Nettie. 'Gregor was driving the car, love.'

15

HARRIET'S LIVING ROOM WAS ALMOST AS PLAINLY furnished and functional as Gregor's: no knick-knacks, no frills and furbelows, but hers had an entirely different vibe. The only ornaments dotted around the room were trophies, twenty or so, awarded by the American Women's Baseball League and the American Women's Baseball Federation. On one wall hung a large black-and-white photograph of a much younger Harriet in action: her body balanced, her right foot solidly on the ground, and her arm following through after having released the ball. The photographer had captured the throw just as the ball had left her hand. Another wall was dominated by a seventy-inch flatscreen TV. The sofa, reclining chair, coffee table, bookshelf and matching chest of drawers were crammed together into one half of the room to make space for the computer setup that Sylvia referred to as 'Mission Control'.

Harriet looked like a little child as she sat in a capacious black leather chair in front of the state-of-the-art system on her enormous desk. Two huge monitors were reflected in her glasses. She looked relaxed, at home and in her element. Sylvia was in her wheelchair to one side and Francine was standing behind Harriet's chair, scowling at the screen in concentration. The pair were distinctly less comfortable than Harriet in this environment.

Harriet pointed at one of the screens. 'So, you've seen the numbers. We're getting there, but not fast enough. I've sourced a local knitwear manufacturer to help us with the mass market knitting items that don't require the personal touch, and that'll really help us on production, but as far as sales are concerned, we need a different angle, something new and dynamic, and we need big orders. We need to get things in the delivery pipeline. These one-off orders aren't going to do it.'

Francine nodded and then let out a deep sigh. 'It feels as though we've sold to everyone we can. Word of mouth can only go so far.'

Harriet nodded. 'Market saturation, dear. That's why we need to think outside the box. We've picked all the low-hanging fruit. Now we need to sprinkle our magic wider.'

'Sprinkle our…? Fucksake, hen – sorry, Francine – this is Janus Lodge, not fuckin' Hogwarts. Sorry, Francine.' Francine simply shook her head, not even glancing Sylvia's way. Harriet continued to tap away at the computer keys without looking down at them, her eyes fixed on the screen, and Sylvia tapped her shoulder. 'Where do you get all this stuff from, anyway – boxes, low-hanging fruit, throwing elephants at flagpoles and all that shite? Whoops. Sorry, Francine.'

Harriet turned to look at her, pushing her glasses back up her nose. 'What I mean, dear, is that we need to expand.' She looked from Sylvia to Francine as though that explained everything. 'We need to expand our customer base, but we also need to expand our range of products.'

Francine moved away from the back of Harriet's chair and went over to the open window, where a thin blind swayed gently in the breeze. 'But what else can we do? We're already knitting and crocheting everything that can possibly be knitted and crocheted. Even if we have this manufacturer of yours helping us with the production side, it's not going to be enough. I understand supply and demand, and we simply don't have the demand.'

Sylvia groaned and rested her forehead on her palm. 'Not you, too. Who do you pair think you are? Milton Keynes?'

Harriet ignored the comment and glanced from one to the other triumphantly. Clearly, this was the moment she'd been waiting for. 'Oh no, my dears. We're most definitely *not* knitting everything that can be knitted. I've identified a gap in the market. Look.'

She tapped a few more keys. Francine walked back over to the screens and Sylvia leaned forward in her wheelchair. Harriet sat back and gestured like a Roman Emperor acknowledging an appreciative crowd at the amphitheatre, very satisfied with herself as Sylvia and Francine drew closer, looks of horror dawning on their faces. Francine leaned her head over to one side as though whatever she was looking at would look better upside down. It didn't. Sylvia shuddered. 'I'm not even sure I want to know what the fuck that is,' she said quietly. For once, Francine didn't reprimand her.

Harriet scrolled through several images. As each one appeared on screen, Sylvia winced. Francine let out a small whimper of distress. Harriet gestured theatrically towards the screen, clearly very pleased with herself. 'That, ladies, is our new product line. As they say, sex sells.'

16

All the knitters were gathered in the lounge at Janus Lodge, seated in rows, as if waiting for a play to start. Most of them were busily knitting – these days, those who could, knitted at every opportunity. Some of the non-knitters were also present, having heard there would be an unveiling of a new range of knitted items today. An excited hum ran through the room.

Mr McKee wandered in and hesitated. He surveyed the layout of the room and frowned. This was usually the seating format when a visiting speaker came, and he clearly wasn't expecting one of those today. He pulled a tattered piece of paper out of his cardigan pocket. 'It's supposed to be Crossword Club today. This isn't the way the seats are arranged for Crossword Club.' Archie, sitting next to Loretta near the back, waved him over and patted the chair on his other side. McKee hesitated, then walked over and sat down next to Archie. 'It's supposed to be Crossword Club today. I've come down for Crossword Club. This seating's not right. This is the seating for presentations.'

'Crossword Club's been cancelled.'

McKee's shoulders stiffened. 'Cancelled? Crossword Club? But it's here.' He held out the monthly events timetable he was holding in his hand. 'See? Two o'clock. Lounge. Crossword Club. They can't cancel Crossword Club.'

Archie smiled at him. 'Well, they have, pal. No Crossword Club today, something *much* more important.'

McKee stared at him blankly. 'What's more important than Crossword Club? It'd better not be some shitey wee talk about the Tudors again. If I have to hear one more time how Henry VIII—'

Archie put a finger to his lips. 'Shhh! They're just about to start.'

Harriet and Francine were standing at the front of the room and Sylvia was in her wheelchair just off to one side. On the table in front of Harriet and Francine stood a large cardboard box. Francine pointed at the flipchart behind her. 'So, as you can see from the figures Harriet's prepared, while we're now at around £500,000 in profit, we've still got a long way to go and only a couple of months left to raise the balance. So, we needed to come up with something drastic.' She looked at Sylvia, who folded her arms and grinned. She was very much looking forward to what would happen next. Francine, on the other hand, cleared her throat nervously. 'So, after investigating the market, and – according to Harriet – done some blue sky thinking, we've come up with a few items and knitted some prototypes.'

She delved into the box in front of her and brought out a bright red knitted item, which she held up to a sea of puzzled faces. She shook it and said brightly, 'Willy warmer.' The faces remained puzzled, and Francine clearly decided to plough on rather than explain further, and hurriedly reached into the box again and pulled out two small and delicate crocheted items made of white and silver wool, round, with long dangling parts. 'And these are... nipple tassels.'

The faces in front of her looked even more puzzled. Sylvia put out her hand and took the nipple tassels from Francine. She placed them in front of her chest and circled her shoulders, making the tassels twirl rather expertly around in circles. At the same time, she duh-duh-duh-DUHed the stripper theme for a few moments before stopping again since – from the rows of blank faces in front of her – it obviously wasn't helping. 'Look, just imagine my nipples were still in their proper place.'

Light began to dawn on the faces of the few men in the room. There were a few exclamations of 'Oh' and 'Ah!' and several knowing nods. The women still looked puzzled, on the whole.

Francine pulled some more knitted and crocheted items from the box and held them up one by one, holding them out so that everyone could get a good look, naming the items as she did so. 'Restraints… knitted handcuffs… knitted whips…' She cracked one of the whips to demonstrate and a woman at the front clutched her chest. Francine held out a calming hand. 'Oh, sorry, Alice.' She reached back into the box, continuing to pull out item after item. '…ticklers… bondage accessories… bondage ropes…'

Thomas Lamont nudged Ailsa in the ribs and winked at her. She blushed and giggled. Francine took a look at the faces in front of her. They were all riveted on her now. Clearly, light was beginning to dawn. She delved back into the box for the *pièce de résistance*. She glanced over at Sylvia, who nodded reassuringly at her, and then pulled out a black, knitted mask. It had silver zips where the eyes would be, and another, larger zip where the mouth would be. She held it up so that everyone could see it in all its full, hideous glory.

Nettie fluttered a hand up to her mouth. 'Dear God, please tell me that's some sort of balaclava.'

Francine shook her head apologetically. 'No. It's a…' She fumbled for the appropriate word and looked over at Sylvia for help.

Sylvia was grinning from ear to ear. 'Gimp mask, dollface. It's what's known as a gimp mask.'

There was a moment of awed silence and then an excited hubbub broke out. The residents crowded around the big box. They pulled out various fetish items – cuffs, collars, ticklers, blindfolds, even a knitted straitjacket. At first, each new article was greeted with looks of shock and squeals of horror. Gradually, however, there were giggles and shrieks of glee. Some of the residents even started trying things on. Harriet beamed at Sylvia and Francine. Mr McKee looked in puzzlement at his timetable and left the room.

17

Sylvia's wheelchair was pulled up close to the computer desk in Harriet's flat and she was furiously tapping away at the keyboard. On the multiple screens, various windows were open: email, Instagram, Facebook, Bluesky, TikTok. Little messages were popping up in boxes everywhere. Sylvia was humming tunelessly as her index fingers plonked down onto the keys. So far, she could only manage to type with her index fingers, but she was getting faster at that.

The outside door of Harriet's flat opened and Harriet's halting steps came up the hallway. 'Sylvia? Are you *still* here?'

Sylvia didn't turn, but carried on typing as she answered rather distractedly, her eyes glued to the screen. 'Aye. Catching up on messages, doll. What's up?'

Harriet entered the room, followed by Jake. 'I met Jake in the hall. He said you've been busy for days on end and haven't had time for him or his dad.' Her voice was suddenly scolding. 'We talked about this before, Sylvia. You've become an internet junkie. It's not good for you.' Sylvia snorted, but continued typing furiously. Harriet hobbled over to her and gently took the mouse from her hand. 'You see people like you on the telly – gamers who never go out of the house, women who get hooked on internet bingo. I'm beginning to regret teaching you all these things.'

Jake stepped forward and bent down to give his gran a kiss on the cheek. 'I'm amazed. You look quite the expert there, and all these years I thought you only wanted to look up dead film stars and see how much they were worth when they died.'

Sylvia continued tapping away without looking round. 'Not just dead ones.' Her voice was absent-minded. 'Did you know that Alan Alda's worth fifty million dollars? They're repeating *M*A*S*H* on one of my channels at the moment. Four episodes a day; it's great.' She swung her wheelchair around and ran a hand over her eyes. 'I've been at this for ages. Harriet's right, this social networking malarkey does hook you in. I'm Facebooked oot ma tits, I tell you.'

Jake covered his mouth to hide his grin. Harriet lowered herself into a chair and groaned. 'I've created a monster.'

Sylvia nodded at the screen, proudly. 'That's us got nearly a hundred thousand friends on Facebook, Harriet. And over that on Insta, since that footballer started following us. An' the Tickety-Tock's gone mad since I started doing those wee videos that you showed me how to make.' She turned back to the screen and peered at it for a second. 'I tell you what, though, since we started selling that new line of sex stuff, we're getting some really kinky followers. I've been learnin' all sorts.'

Jake groaned. 'Oh God, I'm not sure I want to know.'

The computer gave a beep and a message box popped up. Sylvia read it and then poked a finger at the screen. 'This one, for example. This is a message from BigPrinceAlbert1786.'

Harriet gasped and clapped her hands in excitement. 'Royalty? We're getting messages from royalty, Sylvia? How exciting is that? The Royal family is buying our things? Prince Albert of where? Does he say? Is it Monaco? Oh, do say it's Monaco.'

Jake groaned once more and put his head in his hands. Sylvia looked at Harriet pityingly and shook her head. 'Naw, hen. A Prince Albert isn't a member of the Royal family; it's a kind of piercing.'

Harriet looked puzzled. 'Piercing? How do you mean – piercing? As in a piercing cry?'

Sylvia thought for a moment. 'Well, aye, that's the sort of cry you might give if your privates were being pierced, aye.'

Jake gave a whimpering moan. Harriet was still looking puzzled. 'You mean…?'

'Aye, hen. BigPrinceAlbert1786 has had his bits pierced, and so, apparently, have…' she looked carefully at the numbers in his username, '...one thousand, seven hundred and eighty-five other BigPrinceAlberts.' Harriet stood open-mouthed for a second and Jake sank down onto the sofa, holding his ears and continuing to moan as if to drown out the conversation. Sylvia fiddled with the computer mouse. 'Here, he sent me a photo earlier. Come and have a wee swatch.'

Harriet hesitated a moment, but her curiosity eventually got the better of her. She leaned in towards the screen and gasped. Both their heads tilted to one side simultaneously. There was a moment's awed silence. The only movement in the room was Jake, shaking his head as he held it. Harriet straightened up, her head still tilted on one side. 'Do we actually knit things in that size? What is it he wants, anyway?'

Sylvia maximised the message and peered at it short-sightedly. 'Let's see... Hmmm... well, for a start, he says he wants to stick his big, fat—'

'Gran!' Jake's voice was plaintive.

18

GRINDER MAHONEY PULLED UP SLIGHTLY BEFORE THE Springfield Road bookies and parked on the opposite side of the road. PJ was in the passenger seat and Declan sat behind Grinder in the back seat. 'Declan, either shut your mouth or move over and sit behind PJ.'

Declan's mouth opened wider as he contemplated Mahoney's words. 'Eh, boss?'

'Your breathing's annoying me. Move over.'

Declan inched across the leather seat, a hurt look on his face. 'What we doin' here anyway, boss?'

'We're watching.'

Declan leaned further forward. 'What we watchin'?'

PJ turned round and swatted him over the ear. 'The bookies, o' course, big man.' There was silence in the car as they all continued to stare out of the window. PJ's brow furrowed. 'Why *are* we watchin' the bookies, though, boss? It's one of ours.'

Grinder gave a self-satisfied smile. 'Just checking that prick Lamont has done as I asked and got rid of the security guard. He was bleating on about it not being safe, and that we're opening ourselves up to robberies if we do that.'

PJ nodded. 'Oh, aye, right.' He picked at one of the angry-looking spots on his cheek. 'Was he right, boss? *Are* we openin' ourselves up tae robberies?'

Grinder gazed out of the window at the door of the bookies. 'Mahoney's' was emblazoned over the top in red, white and blue. An elderly man came out, clutching a handful of betting slips which he tucked carefully into a pocket before setting off up the road with cautious steps, head down against the wind. 'Yes, he was actually.'

PJ frowned and looked at Declan, who shrugged. 'Then why did you do that, boss? Make Mr Lamont get rid of Big Stevie, I mean?'

Grinder continued to stare out of the window. 'I know what you meant, PJ.'

When Grinder didn't elaborate, PJ looked at Declan again. 'But if anyone finds out, we might get robbed, boss.'

Grinder turned and looked at him, smiling broadly. 'And that would be a shame, wouldn't it, PJ?'

PJ blinked. 'Aye. Aye, it would, boss… wouldn't it?' His voice was confused.

There was an excited snuffling from the back seat. Grinder flicked a glance at the rear-view mirror. 'Good boy, Declan. You've got it, haven't you?' Declan nodded. 'Then why don't you enlighten PJ here.'

Declan leaned forward into the gap between the two seats, breathing heavily. 'We're gonnae rob our own bookies, right, boss?'

Grinder turned the key in the ignition. 'Exactly right, Declan. That's *exactly* what you two are going to do.' He pulled the car smoothly away from the kerb.

19

Janus Lodge's residents and staff were crammed into the small, windowless cinema room. DVDs were neatly stacked on shelves all along the back wall and comfortable cinema-style seats formed two rows at the front of the room. Lydia Wheelan had brought in extra chairs for the occasion and the popcorn machine had been moved into the hallway. Everyone was chattering away excitedly, apart from Gregor Abercrombie, who was standing quietly on his own at the back of the room, leaning against one of the DVD shelving units. The large-screen TV on the wall was tuned to the morning breakfast show. As the credits rolled, the camera moved to a long L-shaped red sofa with a table in front of it containing the day's newspapers, a jug of orange juice, croissants – the usual trappings of a shiny, happy breakfast TV studio.

The hosts, a young blonde woman in a figure-hugging blue dress and a middle-aged man in a grey suit, beamed out of the screen with expansive and expensive smiles. On the screen behind them the Janus Knitwear logo appeared. It had been designed by Harriet: the two-faced god, Janus, expertly rendered in wool by Francine, with a pair of crossed knitting needles in the foreground. Nettie said excitedly, 'Shhhhhh, we're on!'

The honeyed tones of the young woman on screen introduced the film. 'In a moment, we're going to speak to the masterminds behind Janus Knitwear. But first, our cameras were out across Scotland yesterday, filming this latest internet sensation. Let's have a look.'

The film was a montage of people wearing Janus Knitwear

products: the first scene showed a group of bikers pulling onto a petrol station forecourt to fill up with petrol. They took off their helmets and rested them on the seats of their powerful motorcycles as they filled their tanks. Underneath the helmets, every last one of the bikers was wearing a baby-blue woollen balaclava with a red skull and crossbones knitted into the back. Loretta squealed. 'Look! There's Jake!'

The second scene was of a group of hillwalkers striding out along the West Highland Way, kitted out in sweaters, scarves and gloves of the colourful, intricate kind knitted by Francine. Even the little dog running along behind them was wearing a knitted wool coat. The scene changed. In a hospital ward full of incubators, a nurse was checking on the babies as they all slept peacefully. In each incubator was a baby covered by a badly knitted baby blanket in pale blue. Even the baby girls had pale blue blankets. A chorus of 'oohs' and 'ahs' ran around the cinema room and Nettie beamed proudly.

The screen cut away to a market stall apparently doing a roaring trade in knitted goods, with a substantial crowd gathered around it. A sign over the top of the stall proclaimed it to be JANUS KNITWEAR. 'Look! It's us!' Behind the stall stood Loretta and Archie. Knitted handbags were hanging from the top of the stall and sweaters, cardigans, throws, blankets, cushion covers, sets of scarves, gloves and hats were piled up on the stall itself. The crowd of customers, five deep, was clamouring to pay for the items.

In a hen rescue centre in the Scottish Borders, a number of hens were happily pecking at the ground. The voiceover proclaimed them to be ex-battery hens. Their feathers were missing and they looked scrawny and scraggy. Each one of them was wearing a tiny knitted jumper in various colours and different types of wool. Needless to say, there was a preponderance of baby blue.

The final scene was a fetish club in Glasgow. It was dark and the music was pumping. Framed by the darkness and the strobe lighting, a couple were kissing. As they parted, they re-zipped the zips over the mouths of their woollen masks and began dancing again. The scene widened to include other clubbers. A man in a straitjacket made of wool was being led around by a woollen lead, attached to a woollen collar, by a woman wearing a rubber outfit trimmed with wool. In her free hand she carried a woollen whip.

As the scene faded out, the camera returned to the two television hosts. The man smiled. 'Well, wasn't that something? And we're delighted to have with us today three of the lovely ladies who started Janus Knitwear.' The camera panned out to show Francine and Harriet on the sofa, and Sylvia in her wheelchair. Harriet was nervously pushing her glasses up her face, almost disappearing into the huge sofa. Francine was looking regal and composed, as usual. As the TV camera widened to include them, Sylvia reached out and grabbed a croissant from the plate on the table and took an enormous bite. Crumbs fell down to her chest and she brushed them away. They scattered onto the young woman host of the programme. Sylvia reached over to brush them off the host's tight skirt and the woman batted her hand away, still smiling widely for the camera, professional but a tad flustered.

The male host continued. 'Francine Ure, Sylvia Abercrombie and Harriet Knox are trying to save their old people's home—'

Sylvia mumbled through her croissant. 'Haw. It's no' an old people's home, it's a retirement community. We all have our own flat, an' that. It's no' like we're all decrepit.'

'I'm sorry. Retirement community. Now, tell me, why did you feel the need to do this? What are you saving your… community from, exactly?'

Sylvia wiped her mouth with the back of her hand. 'A wee shitebag called Fergus Lamont and his pal, some sort of gangster called Mahoney. They want to knock the place down and build—'

The host held out a hand to stop her. His other hand was on his earpiece, and he was looking flustered. 'We… errrr… do, of course, need to make it clear that there is no evidence this Mr Mahoney is a gangster. The opinion of Mrs Abercrombie is nothing to do with this channel.'

'Aye, whatever. I assume you're not disputin' the fact that Fergus Lamont is a wee shitebag, though?'

The host listened to his earpiece once more. 'And we apologise to our viewers for Mrs Abercrombie's use of bad language.'

'Bad language? You think that was bad language? I can do—'

The young woman smoothly interrupted Sylvia mid-flow. 'Now, who was it that came up with the idea of knitting?'

Francine, Harriet and Sylvia all looked at each other. Francine smoothed her skirt. 'Well, it was a joint idea, really. A lot of us at Janus Lodge knit. And, in fact, there are now more of us who do so, as residents have joined us in our quest to save Janus Lodge. Almost the whole community now knows how to knit, and even those who don't knit have helped in one way or another.'

The male host beamed. 'Splendid! And how much money have you raised to save your… errr… retirement community so far?'

Francine looked at Harriet, who thrust a piece of paper at her, clearly not wanting to speak herself. 'So far, we've raised just over two million pounds. Unfortunately, we need to raise three and a half million, and now have less than two months to do it in. But we're optimistic. We won't rest until we've done everything we can.'

Harriet raised a tentative hand. 'We're also looking for companies who might consider going into partnership with us. We need to be bigger, we need to be quicker, and we need an influx of cash. So, if any of your audience are interested in backing us, we'd be delighted to discuss terms.'

Sylvia nodded. 'Aye. We need one o' they wee horsey things on the chess board.'

The hosts looked at her and then at each other, confused. Harriet leaned forward. 'She means a white knight.'

The female host tapped Sylvia on the knee. 'Of course, dear.' Sylvia looked down at the hand and crossed her arms, and the female host removed it swiftly. 'And whose idea was the… errr… fetishwear?'

Harriet raised her hand again. 'That was me. After investigating the marketplace, it seemed that bondage wear was a market worth exploiting, and we decided to drill down into that demographic.'

Sylvia put a hand over her mouth and coughed to hide a snigger. She then reached out for another croissant and took a huge bite.

'I… see. And do your knitters know what it is that they are knitting?'

Sylvia stopped chewing and looked at her. 'Hen, we might be old, but we've all got eyes, most of us have still got our marbles, and we've all had sex before.' Her voice became wistful. 'Some of us used to have plenty… We're no' all senile, sittin' around in our own pish all day watchin' *Judge Judy*.'

The male host hurriedly broke in. 'And now, the weather…'

20

FERGUS LAMONT THREW THE TV REMOTE ACROSS the table in the walnut-clad boardroom of Prometheus Holdings as the segment on Janus Knitwear came to an end. 'Shit!' The remote landed on the table and skidded to a halt, leaving a six-inch gouge in the shining wood. Lamont lashed out and batted the remote off the table.

The door opened and his secretary came in, carrying his mobile phone as if it were a shite dipped in treacle. 'It's Mr Mahoney, Fergus.' She looked down at the floor, which was now littered with the pieces of the broken remote control.

'Oh God.' He reached out for the phone, holding it away from his ear as if it were radioactive. 'Grinder. How are you?'

'A gangster, Fergus? A fucking *gangster*?'

Lamont stood and pushed his way past his secretary, gesturing at her to pick up the pieces of the broken remote. 'And they called me a wee shitebag, Grinder. I'm not exactly coming out smelling of roses in all this, you know.'

'I'm hurt, Fergus, I have to admit.' Lamont shivered. He knew that the man's understated calmness masked violence and menace. 'Those old fogies are sullying my reputation. That old bag was about to spill the beans about my high-class gentlemen's club. Good job that TV bint interrupted her. I mean, where would we be if that gets out? How does she know what I'm planning to build, anyway?'

Fergus loosened his tie and ran a finger around the inside of his shirt collar as he stepped inside his office, closing the door behind him. 'Not from me, I can assure you.' The noise Grinder made in response was not reassuring, and Fergus swallowed the ball of acid in his throat. 'But look, Grinder, this'll be old news by tomorrow. Besides, they're clearly not going to be able to raise the funds. You heard what they said.'

Lamont could hear the controlled exhalation at the other end of the phone. 'They also said they were optimistic. What the fuck does that mean, Fergus? You need to find out what they've got planned and put a stop to it.'

'But how—?'

'And did you do as I told you and get rid of the security guard at Springfield Road?'

The acidic knot in his belly tied itself even tighter. Fergus sat down at his desk, opened one of the drawers and pulled out a bottle of indigestion medicine. He expertly unscrewed the top with one hand and chugged half of the bright pink liquid down, before returning it to the drawer where it chinked against the others nestled there. 'Not yet. Look, are you sure this is a good idea? It'll be clear to the punters that there's no security and it'll leave the place vulnerable. What if something goes wrong?'

'Well, that would be a shame, wouldn't it, Fergus? Now, go and do some damage control. I don't want everyone thinking I'm some sort of lowlife scumbag gangster.'

'But you—'

Fergus realised he was talking to himself.

21

THE COMMUNITY ROOM AT JANUS LODGE HAD become the centre of manufacturing operations. Several residents – including Sylvia, Nettie, Francine, Loretta and Archie – were manically knitting away, chatting from time to time as they worked. Big piles of wool and finished products were everywhere in the room. There was a sense of organised chaos. Harriet was overseeing things, the ubiquitous iPad in her gnarled hands.

Gregor Abercrombie was sitting in a corner by himself, reading a paper. Every now and again he sneaked a longing look at everything that was going on and the camaraderie in the room which he wasn't part of. Sylvia glanced at him from time to time. On one occasion she started to wheel her way over towards him, but then seemed to think better of it.

A postman staggered in carrying a huge box. On the side, in big letters, was emblazoned: 'DEVIANT DUNGEON – ENJOY THE PAIN'. The postman put the box on the floor and looked at the residents curiously. He held out a machine for someone to sign for the box and Harriet signed it with a flourish. The postman took a final look around the room, then at the box, shook his head and walked out.

Harriet pulled an overstuffed keyring out of the pocket of her cardigan. As well as numerous memory sticks, it also had a Swiss Army knife attached, a red SwissChamp, with thirty-three attachments. It had been a Christmas present from Sylvia and was one of Harriet's prized possessions. She expertly opened out the largest blade, cut the tape on the box and opened the lid. Putting a gnarled hand in, she pulled out a sheet of paper. In big letters at the top, under the Deviant Dungeon logo, 'FREE SAMPLES – FOR YOUR ~~ENJOYMENT~~ PAIN' was typed in bold letters. Underneath was a handwritten note: 'We saw you on the telly and wondered if you might like to consider a partnership.' Harriet waved the piece of paper. 'Here, look at this, it's from a company that wants to work with us.' She put her hand back into the box, reaching through the packing peanuts for the items within.

The residents all stopped knitting to watch. With a flourish, Harriet held up each item for inspection as she lifted it out, reading out the description on the label as she did so: a spanking skirt, latex shorts, PVC gloves, a red PVC nurse's uniform, a men's rubber catsuit, a ball gag, a pink leather collar and chain, several different types of vibrators and dildos. When she held up a bright pink, sparkly, rabbit-style vibrator, Sylvia laughed. 'Harriet, doll, you look a bit like the Statue of Liberty in someone's very weird dream.'

No one else said anything. Eyebrows were raised to the roof and mouths were opened wide. Even Gregor moved closer to take a look. Harriet jumped as she accidentally pushed a button and the rabbit switched itself on with a loud buzzing noise. She dropped it on the floor, where it continued to throb and buzz and its little ears continued to twitch. Everyone watched it for a few seconds and then Nettie slowly bent down to pick it up. She touched the vibrating ears of the rabbit, gave a little squeal and hurriedly handed it over to Archie, who was standing next to her. He touched the ears and his eyebrows raised. A little smile appeared on his face and he passed the rabbit to Loretta, gesturing for her to touch the ears. She put out her fingers and gently did so. Loretta looked at Archie, her eyes widened, and she took the rabbit from him. She put the ears to her nose. As everyone's gaze turned back to where Harriet was pulling the last item out of the box, Loretta quietly turned the rabbit off and slipped it into her handbag.

Harriet hauled out a rubber sleeping bag and let it unravel. 'This looks like a bit of a tight fit. I can't imagine going camping with this.'

The bag had two zips running down the front and a drawstring around the neck. She held it up triumphantly.

'What in holy hell is that?' Sylvia wheeled herself closer to get a better look. 'A heavy-duty dustbin bag?'

Harriet looked at the tag attached to the bag and read it out. 'It says: "Latex Sleep Sack – for a Rubbery Night's Sleep".' She gasped and looked up at them. 'Two hundred and twenty-five pounds! Can you believe it? For a sleeping bag made of rubber. Why on earth…'

Francine cautiously reached out and touched it. 'It would be very hot in there, wouldn't it? Staff insist on Mr Walsh in number 32 having a sheet like this on his bed all the time. I bet that doesn't cost anywhere near as much.'

Nettie tutted. 'No, you can get them for £14.95 from the Co-op.' They all looked at her. 'Erskine needed one a couple of years ago.'

Erskine blushed as they all turned to face him. 'Enlarged prostate, that's all. I'm fine now.'

Sylvia turned back to her knitting. 'Well, most of this stuff's no good to us, is it? Put it back in the box and I'll get Jake to stick all that in my spare room, until we decide what's to be done with it. Maybe we can sell it. By the way, Loretta, doll, don't think I didn't notice you slip that wee pink vibrating thing in yer bag.'

22

Gregor Abercrombie opened the door of the bookie's and nodded to the woman in the wee office behind the safety glass at the counter. 'Morning, Agnes.' The elderly woman lifted her elbows off the counter and pulled her eyes away from the little TV in the corner of her wee cubby hole. Gregor glanced up at the screen she was watching and shuddered. As usual, some smug-faced nyaff was showing a smirking couple around a house that was clearly out of Agnes's price range. He glanced at his watch. Eleven o'clock. No matter what time of the day he came in, Agnes always managed to find this shite on one channel or another. 'Quiet in here today, isn't it?' Gregor took a slip and a stubby pencil out of one of the plastic containers lining the walls and put his folded newspaper down on the narrow ledge.

Agnes sighed. 'The usual, these days, Gregor. Everyone's doing their gambling online, it seems.'

'No' me, hen.' Gregor licked the end of the pencil. 'I like to get out and about. It's a wee bit of exercise for me, so it is, walking down here every day.' He pulled up one of the stools that were dotted about the room and heaved himself onto it.

Agnes nodded. 'How's it going wi' all that knitting, anyway? I saw that wife of yours on the telly a couple of days ago.'

Gregor glared. 'Ex-wife, thanks very much. And I don't really know how it's going. I keep out of it all.'

Agnes looked shocked. 'But don't you care about losing your home?'

Gregor pressed his pencil down too hard on the betting slip, breaking off the point. He threw it into one of the bins and pulled another one out of its stand. 'It's not my home. I don't care where I live.' He scanned the screen showing the odds for the next race and scribbled down his bet. He cast around for a way to change the subject. 'Where's Big Stevie? I've no' seen him around this week. He off sick?'

Gregor handed over his betting slip to Agnes, along with two pound coins. She gave a businesslike nod. 'Two pounds on Fancy Pants in the eleven-thirty? Right you are, Gregor. You'll be able to buy one o' these big houses on my programme if that yin comes up.' She put his money in the till and gave Gregor his copy of the slip back before giving a sigh. 'Stevie's been let go.'

'Let go?' Gregor hoisted himself back onto the stool and looked at his watch. Ten minutes before the next race. 'Who's gonnae guard my two-pound stake, then?'

Agnes snorted. 'Aye, well, it's alright for now, I'll look after it. But it's the Old Firm match coming up. We always get a good crowd nipping in from the pub next door to put bets on for that. I'm no' sure how the boss expects me to deal wi' that lot without Stevie.'

Gregor hunkered down and put his fists up in front of him, assuming a fighting pose with his hands in guard position and swaying as if to avoid an opponent. He punched at the air with a quick one-two combo, ducking his head from side to side. 'Want me to come by and help you out, hen?'

Agnes laughed. 'Naw, you're alright, Gregor. Ah'm no' wantin' to be spoilin' ma evenin' waitin' eight hours for an ambulance wi' ye, when one o' they maddies from the pub lamps ye.'

'Ah, well. Don't say I didnae offer.' Gregor turned back to his paper and studied the form for the next race.

23

A POST VAN DREW UP AT THE front door of Janus Lodge. The postman climbed out and went to the back of the van, sighing and shaking his head as he hoisted two sacks of mail out with a grunt. He struggled in through the front doors and heaved both sacks of mail into one of the two supermarket shopping trolleys that were sitting just inside the entryway. He wheeled the trolley up to the door of the communal lounge and glanced in. 'More fan mail, ladies. Ah'm expecting a really big Christmas tip, by the way. Pay for ma bloody back operation.' Erskine scurried over and wheeled the trolley to the big table, where he and Archibald were opening mail and sorting it into piles marked 'Letters', 'Invoice Payments', 'Donations' and 'Other'.

By now, the lounge had completely stopped being a lounge and had turned into a slick business operation. Knitting was taking place in every spare corner and conversation was a low, cheerful hum. At one end of the room, Harriet was sitting at a small desk, equipped with a laptop and printer. She was tapping away feverishly at a calculator on the desk in front of her, humming tunelessly and inputting the results on a spreadsheet. As the tapping and humming became louder, faster and more furious, until she sounded like a tap-dancing bee, the conversations around her and the clacking of knitting needles gradually stopped until everyone else in the room was watching her expectantly.

Finally noticing the quiet, Harriet slowly sat back in her chair with a small wince caused by sitting bent over the desk for so long. She gazed around at everyone through her thick lenses. 'We've done it.' The almost whisper turned into a squeal. 'We've bloody done it. Two days to go. Ya dancer!'

Sylvia wheeled herself over, clutching her chest. 'Fucksake, doll. Try and remember where you are. A shock like that could finish most of us off, you know. We've raised enough, then?'

Harriet looked at her friend and then at the rest of the room. 'More than enough. The buyout's gone through; the deal's finalised. We've sold the business and we've got enough money to buy this place *and* get a new bus for trips out. You can all stop knitting now and never pick up the needles again, if you like.'

Everyone in the room stood up and gathered around Harriet and each other, dispensing hugs and kisses. Thomas and Ailsa Lamont broke into spontaneous – if very tentative – dancing. An elderly voice from somewhere near the back of the room started to warble 'Land of Hope and Glory'.

Sylvia held up a hand. 'None of that old shite. Let's have something a bit more up-to-date.' She broke into a spirited rendition of The Pogues' 'Streams of Whiskey'. After initial looks of shock, the residents grabbed each other and joined Thomas and Ailsa in dancing. Archie made his way to the organ in the corner and started to accompany Sylvia. Lydia and two members of staff rushed in, clearly concerned at the hubbub. As light dawned, they, too, joined in the dancing. Erskine grabbed Nettie and whirled her into a waltz. Lumpy pale-blue baby blankets flew out of the knitting bag Nettie was still holding and the dancers stomped all over them.

Sylvia watched everyone from her wheelchair and smiled. Everyone seemed suddenly younger, more carefree, all aches and pains gone. She spotted Gregor standing quietly just outside the door of the lounge, one hand on the frame, as if debating whether to cross the threshold. Sylvia's hand fluttered upwards, starting to beckon him in, but he didn't look in her direction. Instead, he turned on his heel and walked away, his shoulders slumped.

Sylvia followed him out, negotiating her wheelchair through the dancers. 'Gregor, why don't you come and join us?' Her voice was tentative but friendly. He stood with his hand on the handle of the door to his flat for a moment, and then, without turning to look at her, he turned the handle and went inside.

'Oh, please yourself, you old misery.' Sylvia shrugged and turned back to the communal lounge, frowning. The dancing had moved out of the lounge and into the corridor, and Nettie and Erskine were now dancing slowly cheek to cheek. The troubled frown on Sylvia's face melted away and she smiled. She wheeled herself to the side of the corridor to watch the dancing, reached into the capacious bag on her lap, and pulled out a can of Guinness.

24

FERGUS LAMONT WAS TROUBLED. HE SAT WITH his feet up on his desk, his arms behind his head, and wondered what he was going to do. The door opened and Fergus opened his mouth to berate Jodie for not knocking, but it was Grinder who strode in, followed by PJ and Declan. Bringing up the rear was Fergus's flustered-looking secretary, her face pink and furious. 'Ah tell't them, Fergus. Ah tell't them you were busy, but they wouldnae wait.' Her voice, when ruffled, lost its honeyed tones and perfect diction.

Fergus took his feet off the desk and nervously waved Grinder to a chair, which the other man ignored. 'No problem, Jodie. As you know, I'm always happy to see Mr Mahoney. Now, fetch these gentlemen some coffee, will you?'

Grinder waved a hand. 'No need, Fergus, no need. This isn't a social call.' Fergus shuddered. Mahoney's voice was the sound of bovver boots on ice-covered gravel. 'We don't want coffee, do we boys?'

'Actually, ah widnae mind a nice cuppa tea, boss.' Declan sniffed and wiped his nose on his cuff. Only then did he look at Grinder and immediately paled. 'Naw, naw, we're awright, cheers, Mr Lamont. Ah'm no' thirsty efter aw.'

Fergus waved Jodie out of the room. As she left, she shot a look at Grinder, as if to make it clear that he wasn't her favourite person. Fergus made a note to speak to her later about that. It never did any good to antagonise Grinder at the best of times, and this was certainly not the best of times.

As if to underline his thoughts, Grinder spoke quietly. 'I'm not keen on that secretary of yours, Fergus. Too fond of taking liberties, it seems to me.'

'Sorry, Grinder.' Fergus wasn't sure why he was apologising, but Grinder Mahoney always made him feel nervous, even though he, Fergus, was clearly his superior socially, intellectually, culturally, sartorially. He brushed a speck of dust off his Armani suit and gestured his visitor towards a chair. 'So, to what do I owe this pleasure?'

'I've just come to see how we're moving along with that wee bit of business, Fergus, my boy.' Fergus bristled at the term but said nothing. Grinder reached out and picked up a trophy from the desk – a golfer wielding a golf club. It was one of Fergus's favourites. He'd won it the previous year in a prestigious competition at his club.

'Well, there's been a wee bit of a hitch, Grinder, but nothing to trouble yourself about.'

To Fergus's dismay, Grinder started twirling the golf trophy by the outstretched club. 'Aye? Is that right? What sort of a hitch?'

Fergus watched the trophy as it spun. 'Nothing major, I'm sure. It seems that the old folks have managed to come up with the cash. Could you please stop...?'

Grinder twirled the trophy faster. 'Three and a half million, that's what we agreed, right, Fergus?'

'Errr... aye... three and a half million, that's right.' Fergus was relieved when Grinder put the trophy carefully back down, but before he knew what was happening, his face was squashed down on his desk, the trophy's golf club inside his nose, looking up at the ceiling with Grinder's face hovering above him, one hand tightly around his throat.

'D'you think I'm stupid, wee man?' Fergus let out a strangled cry and started pointing to his throat, unable to breathe. 'What's that, Fergus? What do you think, boys? Is Mr Lamont here trying to take the piss?' PJ said nothing and gazed at his fingernails, and Declan was jumping up and down excitedly. As Fergus wheezed and turned red, Grinder eased off the pressure on his throat very slightly, but only to take a letter out of the inside pocket of his cashmere coat. He waved it in front of Fergus's sweating face. 'First we agree on three million, then you increase the price to three and a half, and now you write me a letter saying it's four. That's just pure greed, is it no'?'

Fergus turned his head to one side, wheezing and gagging and trying to catch his breath. When he eventually managed to speak, his voice was raw and hoarse. 'I must…' He coughed. 'Jodie must have made a mistake typing up the letter… you've got…' He wheezed and coughed again. '…the wrong end of the stick. It's three and a half… as agreed.'

Grinder hauled him up by the throat until their faces were only centimetres apart. 'Naw, I think it's *you* that's got the wrong end of the stick, Fergus. It's no' three and a half mill after all.'

Fergus shook his head, confused, and rubbed at his neck, very carefully. 'It's not?'

Grinder sighed and shook his head, as if desperately sad. 'No, Fergus. I think you'll find that the property market has taken a slump in the last wee while. The property's only worth two and a half million to me now.' He finally released Fergus fully. As Fergus struggled to sit up on his own, Grinder straightened his tie for him, very gently.

'Two and a… but we agreed…'

'Aye, we did agree, right enough, indeed we did, Fergus. And then you reneged on our deal and said the price had increased. So, I think you'll find that all bets were off at that point.'

'But…' Lamont shook his head, trying to clear his thoughts. 'The residents have agreed to three and a half. I'm not going to accept two and a half.' He suddenly remembered a much bigger issue. 'Besides, they have first refusal. And they've raised all the funds, so it looks like we've got a problem here after all.' A feeling of relief came over him. Whatever happened, he was going to be three and a half million pounds richer.

Grinder smiled, almost kindly, Fergus thought. 'No, we most certainly *don't* have a problem, Fergus.' Grinder nodded at his heavies and turned to leave the room. As he reached the door, he turned back. 'I'm afraid it means that *you* have a problem, Fergus. And, what's more, if you don't get it sorted by the end of the month, the deal's off. And not only that, you owe me three and a half million for breach of contract.'

Fergus was still sitting on his desk. 'Three and a half? But… you said you were only going to pay…'

Grinder pulled on his leather gloves. 'Exactly, Fergus. Exactly.'

25

Sylvia picked up a shiny box from Harriet's desk and turned it over a few times. The neat label, proclaiming it a 'SpyPod LOC-8-OR', didn't help. She nudged Harriet, who was sitting at the desk, staring up at the monitors. The spreadsheets displayed on both of the monitors were reflected in the thick lenses of her glasses. 'What's this, doll?'

Harriet blushed and looked a little sheepish. 'It's a… I bought it before all this started. I thought I was going a bit… senile. Kept misplacing and losing things, you know.'

Sylvia raised her eyebrows. 'Senile? You? You're the least senile person I know.'

Harriet's lip trembled slightly. 'Well, I didn't want to worry anyone, but I was concerned that I was going to misplace *myself*. So, I went on the internet and investigated the technological options that might help me. The LOC-8-OR got good reviews, so I bought it.'

Sylvia passed the box over to her. 'What does it do? Show me.'

Harriet opened the box and took out the contents. She held up a smooth black device that looked to Sylvia like a fancy watch. 'You keep this bit with you. Just strap it to your wrist. And then if you get lost…' she reached into the box and held up a second part, bigger, with a screen and buttons, '…this bit locates the thing that's missing. In this case, me.' She looked at Sylvia and her lip wobbled again. 'I was going to ask you if you'd look after that bit for me. Then if I… wandered off or something… you could find me.'

Sylvia reached out and put a hand on Harriet's. 'You're not really worried, hen, are you?'

Harriet shrugged. 'A wee bit, aye.' Her face brightened. 'But less than I was before all this.' She waved a hand at the screens. 'It's been a new lease of life for me, all this business stuff. I'd almost forgotten who I was. Maybe *that's* why I thought I might lose myself, because I already felt as though a part of me was missing.'

Sylvia gazed at her for a moment. 'You've got a mind like a steel trap, doll. There's plenty in here who'll lose their marbles before you do. Including me.' She took both parts of the device from Harriet and looked at them carefully. Then she strapped the watch part to her own wrist with some difficulty and handed the screen part back to Harriet. 'Let's have a game of hide-and-seek.'

26

Lydia Wheelan unfolded and refolded the letter in her hand as she stood nervously outside the doors of the communal lounge. She'd struggled to keep her voice calm when she'd made the announcement over the Lodge's intercom system for everyone to gather in the lounge, and she was struggling now to keep the tears at bay. She needed to keep it together for everyone else's sakes; it wouldn't do if she broke down. She took a deep breath and stepped into the lounge. She was greeted with smiles and hellos. Every available seat was taken, and those residents who could easily stand were doing so. As she entered the room, Gregor Abercrombie slipped in behind her and leaned against the door frame, his usual place at the back of a room so that he didn't need to talk to anyone, his arms crossed, a scowl on his face.

Lydia surveyed the rest of the room. Everyone else was still on a high from the happiness and relief at saving their home, and now she was going to have to spoil it all. She hadn't thought this through. The news she had to impart might, quite literally, kill some of these residents.

Sylvia wheeled herself over to Lydia, frowning. 'What's up, hen? You don't look well.'

Lydia pressed a hand on Sylvia's shoulder. 'Just a bit of bad news, that's all, Sylvia.' She glanced around. 'Is everyone here?' She didn't wait for an answer before raising her voice. 'I'm sorry, everyone, but there's been a bit of a hitch.'

Harriet pushed her glasses up her nose. 'What sort of a hitch?'

There was no way of softening the blow, but Lydia tried. 'Just a bit of a… delay… with the purchase of Janus Lodge. I'm sure it'll be…' Her voice drifted off. She wasn't sure it would be fine at all, and she didn't want to lie to her lovely charges, so she didn't finish her sentence.

'What's happened?' They were gathered around her now.

'There's been some sort of problem with the original legal documents.'

'You mean the ones my father drew up?' Thomas Lamont stepped forward, a frown on his face.

'Yes, I'm sorry, but your son's lawyer has found some sort of… anomaly in the document and now…' Once again, Lydia wasn't quite sure how to finish the sentence.

'And now he's trying to weasel his way out of the sale of Janus Lodge to us?' Thomas's voice was flat.

Lydia sighed and nodded. 'That's about the size of it, yes, I'm afraid so.' A wave of concerned murmuring went through the room. A couple of residents started to cry, and Lydia held out her hands to calm them. 'No, no, please don't worry. I'm sure it can all be cleared up. There'll be a delay, that's all, I'm sure. I've spoken to our lawyer and he's… going to look into it.'

'What did he say, exactly?' Harriet's voice was sharp.

Lydia cleared her throat. 'He said… he said…' Lydia was torn. She didn't want to give them false hope, and she didn't want to lie to them, but she was worried about the effect this might have. 'He said it didn't look good. That although we might, technically, have to be offered the place first, it *doesn't* necessarily mean he has to sell it to us. He says that, on the face of it, Lamont is within his rights to explore other options, according to this clause… Such a tiny, *inoffensive* clause…'

Sylvia broke in. 'So because some dodgy lawyer's found some slippery clause in that document his grandfather drew up, Fergus Lamont thinks he can just destroy all our lives?' She turned to Thomas and Ailsa Lamont, who were looking particularly distressed. 'Can you get that wee bawbag over here? I want to have a wee word wi' him.'

'Sylvia!'

Sylvia glared at Lydia. 'He *is* a bawbag, though.'

'But that's not very *nice*.' Lydia waved a hand towards Fergus Lamont's parents.

Thomas shrugged his shoulders. 'Aye, no worries, hen. He *is* a bawbag right enough.' Ailsa nodded glumly and then burst into tears. Nettie enfolded her into a warm hug.

'Can you, but?' asked Sylvia. 'Get him over here, I mean.'

Thomas was ineffectually patting his wife's shoulder. 'Well, aye, I guess so. Normally he wouldn't take any mind of us, but he sent a message through his secretary that he needs to witness us signing some forms before next Friday, so he'll be keen to hear from us for once, I'm sure.'

Francine sighed. 'He's already made his mind up, though. There's no point in trying to persuade him otherwise and I doubt there's anything we can do or say that would stop him.'

'Is there no'? We'll see about that, doll. That dickhead's not going to throw *us* out of here without a fight back.' And with that, Sylvia expertly spun her wheelchair around and wheeled herself to the door of the room, her face set. Everyone backed out of her way before she mowed them down.

Gregor remained leaning on the door frame and he looked down at Sylvia, his face unmoving. Sylvia glared back at him, her features equally stony. Finally, he stepped to one side, and she wheeled herself past him without a word.

27

THE BOOKIES WAS ALMOST DESERTED. GREGOR WAVED a hand in greeting at Agnes, who was sitting in her wee booth behind the screen as usual, and nodded at two old guys over in the corner. He knew every denizen of this place by sight, but none of them to speak to. He wasn't interested in making friends. He picked up a pen and a couple of betting slips as he made his way to his usual seat, reflecting once more that he was glad the Springfield Road bookies hadn't gone the way of many others and converted to technology. In this case, however, it was because the management probably hadn't wanted to spend the money. He glanced around. This place had looked exactly the same for the last twenty years. It had been his local bookies even before he'd moved to Janus Lodge; it was one of the reasons he'd moved there in the first place, after he was too unfit to manage the stairs at his old flat. He didn't like change and upheaval, never had, so the familiarity of the bookies was balm to his soul. Things were better when they stayed the same. He sighed. If only things *had* stayed the same, he could have spent the last half of his life as happy as he'd been in the first half. He sighed again. This had to stop, it never did any good to think about all that. He pulled out his *Racing Post*, glancing at his watch as he did so. The 12.30 at Chepstow, that's what he needed to concentrate on right now.

He looked down the list of runners. Black Tulip was a possibility, but the odds would be shite. Ariadne's Web had gone off the boil recently, so that one wouldn't do. Sylvia's Fancy… He shook his head. Things always brought him back to the past; he'd leave that race alone. How about the 12.40 at Newmarket? There. Grumpy Old Man. Perfect. He wrote out his slip and took it up to the counter. Agnes reluctantly dragged her eyes away from the TV.

'Alright, Gregor?' She looked at the pound coin he pushed across the counter to her. 'Aye, well, this'll keep us in business, won't it?'

Gregor shrugged. 'You get enough out of me, Agnes, so don't complain. I spend practically my whole pension in here. Not that it does me any good, mind you.'

Agnes laughed. 'Part of the furniture, so you are.'

'Business slow?'

She scoffed and shook her head. 'Rakin' it in hand over fist, that bastard of a boss, despite what it looks like. He had no need to let Stevie go. There's plenty of money comin' in. An' we've got one of our biggest day's takings coming up, too.'

'Old Firm match?'

'Aye. It's always a big money-spinner, but the fact that it's a cup game always makes it an even bigger draw.'

Gregor shrugged. 'Aye, well, I know your boss, Fergus Lamont, his parents live at the Lodge. Never comes to visit them and now he wants to sell the place from under us. I'm not surprised he's got his eye firmly on the bottom line here.'

'Lamont?' Agnes sniffed. 'Naw. He's just the supposedly acceptable face of this place. The real boss is a gangster called Mahoney; he likes to keep it quiet, but he owns a string of bookies and bingo halls and God knows what else, right across the city.'

Gregor picked up his copy of the betting slip that she'd passed through the gap in the plexiglass screen. 'Mahoney? He's the boss, is he? He's the one that wants to buy Janus Lodge, I think.'

'Aye?' Agnes glanced up as the door opened, nodding at the newcomer. 'Well, I hope youse manage to raise the money to buy it. He needs bringing down a peg or two, that one. It would serve him right if someone *did* rob this place. Serve him right for letting go of Stevie.' She motioned Gregor to one side so that she could serve the man who had just come in. 'Anyway, if he ever visits your place, you want to keep well out of his way. He's no' a very pleasant man, to say the least.'

Gregor nodded and shuffled back to his seat to consider the following race.

28

Sylvia's living room was eccentrically furnished, with a hodgepodge of mismatched but homely furniture in bright colours dotted about the room, carefully placed for ease of access for her wheelchair. Well-worn wheelchair tracks on the short pile of the carpet led from room to room. Several vases of cheery flowers and photos, mostly of Jake and his parents, were arranged on every available flat surface. More family photos lined the walls, including a large one of Sylvia and Gregor on their wedding day, seemingly in pride of place.

Fergus Lamont was perched uncomfortably on the edge of the only upright chair in the room. Sylvia wasn't sure why she still kept it; nobody ever sat on it when they visited. She'd shown Fergus Lamont to it with glee when he'd arrived. An open briefcase was on the floor by the side of his chair with a typewritten document lying on top of it. He held a delicate cup and saucer in one hand and a biscuit in the other. He looked around for somewhere to put the biscuit down, but there was nothing within reach; most of the flat surfaces were at the sides of the room, to leave more space for Sylvia. He put the biscuit down carefully on his knee and took a sip of his tea.

Sylvia wheeled her chair towards the kitchen. 'Another wee cup of tea, Mr Lamont?'

Lamont shook his head. 'No, I really must be going, Mrs Abercrombie. I don't know what can be keeping my parents. When you spoke to my secretary on their behalf, you did say they would meet me here at your flat, yes? Why was that? What's wrong with their own place?'

Sylvia avoided the question and smiled reassuringly at him. 'Och, they'll be along soon enough, I'm sure. Probably having a wee bit of nookie somewhere, you know what they're like.' Lamont cleared his throat, embarrassed. Sylvia turned her chair to face him. 'Now, about this sale.'

Fergus looked at his watch. 'I've already made my point, quite clearly, Mrs Abercombie. Now, I really must be going. When my parents get back, please tell them I was here.' He took the biscuit off his knee and placed it on the saucer, and held the cup and saucer out to her. 'I've got an appointment at the lawyers to finalise the sale. It's really very inconvenient of my parents to keep me waiting.'

Sylvia ignored the proffered cup and saucer. 'But don't you need your parents to sign, too? That's what they said.'

'Yes, but it's just a formality. My signature is the one that matters. Besides, I think we can all safely say that my parents are unfit… Anyway, tell them I'll be back for their signatures tomorrow. I need to have it all signed by the end of next week, or the deal's off.' He bit his lip, as if realising he'd said too much, and then turned away, leaning down to put the document in his briefcase.

'Off?' Sylvia brought her wheelchair to a stop right in front of his chair.

Lamont winced as the footrest of the chair knocked against his shin. 'Now, I really must go. Please tell my parents I'm not happy that they kept me waiting like this, and to be sure that they're in tomorrow.' He bent down once more to close his briefcase.

Before she could think about what she was doing, Sylvia reached out and picked up a heavy glass vase full of daffodils from one of the numerous side tables that lined the walls. She brought it crashing down on the back of Lamont's head as he was snapping the briefcase latches firmly shut. He grunted and slid off the upright chair and collapsed on top of his case, surrounded by broken glass and bent daffodils.

29

The hallway was empty. Good. Nobody had heard anything. But now Sylvia was left with a dilemma. She had acted on the spur of the moment when the lifeline of the deal being off if Lamont didn't sign it had been thrown out to her. She'd caught it, but she hadn't considered the consequences of her actions. She needed help. Harriet would know what to do, and would do it without question, but was physically incapable. Francine was physically capable, but Sylvia wasn't sure she would go along with this plan without a lot of persuasion, and they didn't have time for that. Besides, if she refused to be part of it, that would spoil everything. She could phone Jake. He'd help immediately, but she didn't want to get him into trouble. He had his whole life ahead of him; it didn't matter about what was left of hers. She was prepared to go to prison if she had to. She'd watched *Prisoner Cell Block H*. She'd soon be Top Dog. Sylvia looked up and down the hallway and sighed. No, there was only one person she could ask, no matter how much it stuck in her throat to do so. She closed the door firmly behind her – it wouldn't do any good at all for somebody to go wandering into her flat for a chat – and made her way along the corridor.

She stopped outside Gregor's door and hesitated before knocking. It was only a moment before she heard light footsteps approaching the door from the other side. She drew in a wavering breath. Gregor opened the door and his mouth fell open in shock.

'I need your help.'

He looked at her for a moment, and then made as if to close the door again.

'Please… Gregor. I need your help.'

He shook his head and the gap in the open door narrowed. Sylvia wheeled her chair into the space, the footrest of her wheelchair scratching the bright green paint at the bottom of the door.

'Please.'

Gregor opened the door a fraction and looked down at the scratch on his door. 'What?'

'I've told you. I need your help.'

'Why?' He was still refusing to look at her.

'I need you to come with me.'

'Where?'

Sylvia was frustrated. 'For fucksake, Gregor. This isn't Twenty Questions. I need you to come with me. Please. I wouldn't have come but you're the only one I can ask; the only one I can trust.'

This last was said in a quiet voice and Gregor opened the door a smidge wider, but only so he could glare at her properly. 'Your attitude isn't making me any keener to listen to you, you know.'

'I know. I'm sorry.' Sylvia glanced around to make sure there was no one about. It was make-or-break time. 'I'll tell you what, I'll apologise thoroughly for everything I've ever done… after you've helped me with the dead man in my living room, I promise.'

'What?'

'Oh, don't start that again.' She turned away from Gregor's door. 'Now, come and give me a hand with this body, you cantankerous old bastard.'

30

GREGOR WAS BENT OVER THE PRONE FORM of Fergus Lamont. Sylvia, feeling a little light-headed, had remained at the door of the living room. 'Well, *is* he dead?' She couldn't stop the slight waver in her voice.

Gregor knelt on the floor with a groan and felt Lamont's neck. 'I don't think so. No, he's not; I can feel his pulse.'

Now she knew Lamont wasn't dead, Sylvia took pains to seem nonchalant about the whole thing. 'Shame.' She headed towards the kitchen. 'A wee cuppa? Chocolate digestive?' Gregor stared at her, aghast. 'No? Something stronger, maybe? I think I'll have a wee brandy, calm my nerves. Aye, a wee double brandy and dry ginger. I think I've got some ice cubes in the freezer. You sure you won't join me?'

Gregor hauled himself back up to standing and eased out his back. 'Jeez-o, Sylvia. You've just battered a man to death, and you're talking about tea and biscuits and what you're going to put in your brandy as if you're having a tea party.'

Sylvia shrugged. 'I thought you said he *wasn't* dead.' At that very moment, Fergus twitched and groaned, although his eyes remained closed. 'See?'

Gregor moved to the old-fashioned phone on one of the side tables. 'Right, we'd better call an ambulance.' He picked up the receiver.

Sylvia, with great aplomb, whizzed her chair over to him and grabbed the phone out of his hand. 'No!'

'What are you doing, woman?'

Sylvia put the phone back on the table. 'We can't call an ambulance.'

Gregor stared at her, nonplussed. 'How no'? You can just tell them it was a mistake. They'll just think you're a wee bit senile.' He looked at her appraisingly, and then at the twitching body on the floor. 'It's no' as if they'd be far wrong, is it?'

Sylvia wheeled her chair back over towards Lamont, who was starting to snore gently. 'Listen. Before I hit him on the head, he said something.'

'What? "Don't hit me, you mad witch." Was that it?'

Sylvia waved a hand as if batting away an annoying fly. 'No. He said that if the property deal wasn't signed off by the end of next week, then it wouldn't go through.'

Gregor glared at her. 'So?'

Sylvia tutted with exasperation. 'So? What do you mean, "so"? It's obvious. So we need to stop the deal being signed off, that's what's so.'

Gregor raised his eyebrows and scoffed. 'Oh, that's easy then. So… what… we just keep him hostage in your living room until the end of next week?' He laughed and shook his head in mock despair. 'Because that's the logical thing to do, isn't it?'

'Aye, Gregor. That's exactly what we're gonnae do.' The smile on Gregor's face faded as the one on Sylvia's grew wide and bright.

31

HARRIET MADE HER WAY ALONG THE CORRIDOR slowly and painfully, leaning heavily on her stick. She stopped in front of Sylvia's door and had lifted her hand to knock when a thudding noise came from inside. She tried the door, concerned that Sylvia had had some kind of accident, but it was locked. This, in itself, was unusual. Sylvia only ever locked her door at night, before she went to bed, and sometimes she didn't even do that. Harriet put an ear to the door.

'Watch it, Gregor!' Sylvia's voice was sharp. Harriet drew back slightly. Gregor? What was *he* doing in there? As far as she knew, Sylvia and Gregor hadn't spoken in years.

Gregor's voice came in response. 'Sorry. It's the rubber. It's slippery.'

'You need to slide it on from the bottom.' Harriet recoiled in horror and raised a hand to her mouth. Then, unable to resist, she pressed her ear closer to the door and heard a grunt from Gregor.

'Careful!' Sylvia was panting now.

'He's too big.'

Sylvia snorted. 'Don't be ridiculous, you old fool. The rubber stretches. Here, I'll pull it from this side. You get your hand in there.'

Harriet stepped away from the door, her hand to her mouth. She stood for a moment, staring at the door, aghast, and then walked off. She had only taken a few steps when she hesitated, turned back to the door, and put her ear to it once more, just in time to hear Gregor gasp, 'Now what?'

'The bedroom.' Sylvia was gasping too.

Silence followed, broken only by the occasional grunt. Harriet shifted position so that she could get her whole ear to the door. Eventually Gregor's strained voice said, 'This just isn't going to work like this; I don't think we can manage on our own. We need someone else.'

'It'll have to be Harriet.'

Harriet gasped as though she'd been caught out and teetered back from the door, feeling horrified – then put her ear against the door once more. She didn't want to listen, but now she couldn't drag herself away.

Gregor was mid-sentence. '…going to be much bloody good, is she? We need someone fitter.'

Harriet's eyes opened wider.

Sylvia sighed. 'Aye. You're right. She's no' gonnae be much good to us.'

Harriet stepped back from the door, trying to hold back her tears. She tapped off down the corridor. She might not want to be part of… whatever weird games Sylvia and Gregor were playing, but she was hurt all the same.

32

Gregor was dishevelled and red-faced. He groaned as he stood up and rubbed his knees. They wouldn't straighten, and he hobbled over to a chair and eased himself into it. Sylvia glanced down to where Fergus was now zipped tightly up into a rubber sleeping bag, with a ball gag in his mouth and a blindfold over his eyes. 'He's starting to come round.' As if to prove her right, Fergus let out a weak cough.

Gregor leaned over the arm of the chair and stared at him. 'Can he breathe?' he said, dubiously.

'Of course he can breathe. This is top-class fetishwear. It's made for comfort and practicality.'

Fergus tried to cough once more, squirming feverishly in his rubber sleeping bag. Gregor's face was panicked. 'It sounds like he's choking.'

'He'll be fine.' Sylvia turned her wheelchair towards the door. 'Now, you can take the blindfold off and get that gimp mask on him; it'll be more secure, and I'll go and get Francine.'

Sylvia unlocked her door and wheeled herself up to the communal lounge. Unusually, Harriet was the only person there. Equally unusually, she had none of her electronic equipment with her and was simply sitting in one of the big chairs staring into space. As Sylvia entered the room, Harriet looked at her and then turned her face away.

Sylvia was rather taken aback – Harriet was always happy to see her. 'Alright, doll? Have you seen Francine?'

Harriet's voice was aghast. 'Francine?'

'Aye, doll. Gregor and I are in need of her services.'

Harriet turned to look at her once more, her face a picture of unhappiness. 'Services? What do you think she is? Some sort of… sex worker?'

Sylvia was puzzled. 'Eh?' Perhaps Harriet had been right, and her mind *was* going.

A tear appeared on Harriet's powdery cheek. 'Besides, what's Francine got that I haven't?'

'What?'

Harriet looked away again, as if she couldn't bear to look at Sylvia. 'I mean… I'm not jealous or anything, and it's not like I actually want to be involved in your kinky sex games, but it would have been nice to have been asked.'

'Kinky…?' Sylvia didn't know how to finish the sentence.

33

Gregor, Sylvia, Harriet and Francine looked silently down on the rubber-covered body of Fergus, wriggling like a fat, black slug on Sylvia's living room floor.

Harriet screwed up her face and pushed her glasses further up her nose. 'Can he hear us?' Her voice was a nervous whisper.

Gregor shook his head. 'No, he's got one of those…' He looked over at Sylvia. 'I have no idea what that thing you gave me is called.'

Sylvia picked up the empty box. 'Sensory deprivation hood.'

Francine peered at the thing on the floor. 'Why does it have little pink ears on the top like a pig?'

Sylvia sighed. 'Look, I didn't have time to go through all the boxes. It was the first one I pulled out.'

Francine sat down. 'There are more like that?' Her voice was almost a whisper.

Sylvia pointed over at a larger box. 'Aye, it's one of those boxes of rubber things from that Deviant Dungeon place. Farmyard animals collection, according to the packing note: cows, pigs, sheep, horses, goats and chickens.'

Francine looked inside the box. 'Chickens? Do chickens even *have* ears?'

'Oh, for… Do I *look* like David Attenborough?'

Harriet poked the slug with her walking stick and it reacted as if it had been sprinkled with salt, drawing away and curling up, as far as the rubber and buckles allowed. 'Do you think he's alright?'

Sylvia waved a dismissive hand. 'He'll be fine. People do this all the time.' Her voice was airy and they all looked at her. 'I read about it.' Francine raised an eyebrow. 'What? I like to expand my horizons, that's all. Jeez-o, you knock *one* man out and dress him head to toe in rubber…'

Harriet shook her head in exasperation. 'Where are we going to put him?'

'And how long are we going to keep him?' Francine crossed her arms and glared at Sylvia.

Sylvia expertly lifted herself out of her wheelchair and onto the sofa. 'In my spare bedroom. Just until the end of next week.'

'The end of *next week*? How are we going to feed him?' Harriet joined Sylvia on the sofa, sinking down with a groan.

Sylvia waved a hand towards the rubber-clad figure. 'Why do you think gimp masks have zips?'

'What about…?' Gregor drifted off and they all turned to look at him. 'Well… you know…'

Light dawned for Sylvia. 'Jeez-o Gregor. This place is full of old codgers. I'm sure at least one of them has a chamber pot.'

'But how are you going to cope? You can't be lifting him every time he wants a… wee.' Sylvia bit her lip at the delicacy of Francine's terminology.

Sylvia shrugged her shoulders. 'Aye, right enough. An' his hands are tied, too. I'm not touching his…' She waved a hand. 'Gregor will just have to stay here.'

Gregor put his head in his hands and groaned.

34

GRINDER PUT THE PHONE DOWN AND LEANED back in his chair. PJ and Declan had just come into his office and were hovering expectantly in the doorway. He waved them to the seats in front of his desk and they looked at each other – it wasn't often they were offered seats. 'I just phoned his wife. Some woman phoned her three days ago, saying she was his secretary and that he'd been called away on urgent business. But when I phoned his secretary, she said that *she'd* got a call from his wife telling her that he had the flu and wouldn't be in for a week or so. Any news from any of the bookies and bingo halls? Any of them heard from him?'

PJ shook his head. 'Naw, boss. None o' them've seen him either, not for the past three or four days. The Springfield Road bookies said that the last time they saw him, he was putting on his coat, and he told that Agnes he was off to see his parents to get them to sign some papers and that he'd be back later.'

Grinder nodded slowly. 'Aye. That fits with what his secretary told me. He told her he was off to Springfield Road and wouldn't be back that day. So, she wasn't expecting to see him, and then his wife – supposedly – phoned her the next day.' Grinder lapsed into silence.

'Boss?'

Grinder picked up the tub of hand cream on his desk and unscrewed the top, rubbing cream into his hands, deep in thought. 'Aye, PJ?'

'You don't think he's…' PJ frowned, clearly not quite sure how he should broach the topic.

Grinder helped him out. 'Done a bunk? Taking some of our hard-earned cash with him?' PJ bobbed his head, clearly relieved that Grinder had said it first. 'No. I think he'd know better than that, don't you? But no harm in checking. I'll phone round. Make sure the safes are all still full.' He put his elbows on his desk and picked up his phone. 'You two can go and get that car cleaned while I'm doing this, then get yourselves back here and pick me up. I need to get home to change for a dinner at the Conservative Club tonight. Pressing the flesh and calling in some favours.'

PJ and Declan stood up. PJ hesitated. 'Boss?'

'Aye?'

'We gonnae do the Springfield Road job, or what?'

Grinder looked at him thoughtfully. 'I think, at the moment, it's "or what", PJ. Lamont's absence could cause us all sorts of problems. The manager goes missing and then the place is immediately burgled? That might cause us some bother and bring down more heat on us than we can deal with, so we'll hold off on that little plan for now.'

'Aye, but…' PJ was clearly concerned, but hesitant to go against his boss.

'Aye, but what, PJ?'

PJ frowned. It only made him look constipated. 'Security's a bit thin on the ground at the bookies, boss, and people must be noticin'. What if someone beats us to it in the meantime?'

Grinder laughed, softly. 'You think someone's gonnae do that? I don't think that's going to happen, do you? Nobody's going to rob from one of *my* businesses apart from me.' He stabbed a number into his phone. 'Now, go and get that car washed; and then first thing tomorrow morning, if Fergus hasn't turned up, we'll speak to his secretary again to get the full story of what he told her when he rang her from the bookies. And then I think we need to pay a little call on Janus Lodge, since that's the last place we know he was heading for.'

35

The sensory deprivation hood was now lying on the chest of drawers at the side of the narrow single bed in Sylvia's spare bedroom. Sylvia inclined her head at Gregor, and he looked blankly back at her. *Tell him*, she mouthed. *What we said.*

Gregor closed his eyes, a pained look on his face. 'Hey man,' he drawled, in a gruff American accent. 'You promise not to cry out and I'll unzip the gimp mask and remove the ball gag.'

Sylvia glared at him. *What the fuck?* she mouthed, and Gregor shrugged and turned back to the encased body on the bed, which was now emitting strangled grunts and wriggling.

'Is that a promise?' The grunting and wriggling came again. 'Nod your head if you agree.' The American accent had moved from deepest Arkansas to The Bronx via Wales, and Sylvia bit her lip to stop herself from laughing. The head in its gimp mask nodded vigorously and Gregor looked over at Sylvia. She nodded.

Gregor gingerly unzipped the mask and removed the ball gag underneath, then let out a yell and pulled his hand back. 'He bit me! The wee arsehole bit me!' His accent was back to normal.

Sylvia reached over and immediately zipped the mask back up. 'No' a good idea, Fergus. Nobody bites Jack Reacher here and gets away with it.' She looked at Gregor. 'What the fuck was that accent all about?'

Gregor rubbed at his hand. 'We mustn't let him know who we are.'

'Too late for that,' Sylvia said cheerfully. 'The last sight he saw yesterday was me aiming a heavy vase at him. I don't think it would take much brain power to work out who we are. Especially now he's bitten down on your arthritic fingers.' She patted somewhere round about Lamont's shoulder – it was difficult to tell in his awkward situation. 'Isn't that right, Fergus?'

The voice that answered her was muffled by the gimp mask, but, without the ball gag, it was easy to understand. 'I didn't mean it; I was just trying to draw a breath. If you let me go, I promise I won't tell anyone that you kidnapped me.'

Sylvia laughed. 'Oh, that's what they all say, isn't it? And then the next thing you know, you're outside a bank holding a hostage as a shield and shouting "Attica! Attica! Attica! Attica!" and the FBI are crawling all over the place with their guns drawn.'

Gregor stared at her. 'What? Have you lost your mind, woman?'

'Al Pacino in *Dog Day Afternoon.*' She turned back to Lamont, who was still emitting muffled sounds. 'Now, Fergus. Do you promise to be quiet if I unzip this again?'

'Yes.'

'Say, "I promise."'

Lamont sighed. 'I promise.'

'Right. I'm going to unzip the mask, and you'll be quiet, just like you promised, and if you are, I'll put a straw in your mouth and give you a drink. You must be thirsty. Does that sound okay?'

Lamont nodded. 'Yes.'

'How about… "Yes please, that sounds lovely."'

The voice was a muffled squeak. 'Yes please, that sounds lovely.'

Sylvia picked up a water bottle from the bedside cabinet. 'And then if you're really good, I'll make you a wee bite to eat. I've got some nice ham left from my Tesco delivery.' She frowned. 'You're no' a vegetarian or anything like that, are you, Fergus?'

'What? No, I'm not vegetarian you mad old bat. Just give me a—'

Sylvia raised her eyebrows and looked over at Gregor. 'Well, that wasn't very nice, was it, Fergus? I'm a bit hurt. Probably too hurt to give you a wee drink of water. I might just pop this ball gag back on over the gimp mask and leave you to stew for a bit longer.'

As Lamont writhed on the bed whimpering, Sylvia smiled over at Gregor.

'You're enjoying this, aren't you?' Gregor's voice was almost a growl.

Sylvia pondered the question a moment before replying. 'Aye. Aye, I am, actually.'

'He's right, you know. You *are* a mad old bat. I can't believe you've got me into all this.'

Sylvia grinned. 'Oh, get over yourself. This is the most exciting thing that's happened in a long time. Let's leave him for a little while. Another hour or so, thirsty and hungry, might make him a little more amenable. Then we'll put the gag back on and go to bed.' Gregor looked at her, aghast. 'Oh, don't worry. I'm no' propositioning you or anything. I've got a blow-up bed that we can put down for you in here.' She patted Lamont's black rubber casing once more and leaned down to speak into where his ear would have been. 'That'll be nice, won't it, Fergus? I'll warn you though, he snores like a rhino.'

The only response was frantic wriggling and muffled squeals.

36

Lydia ran her hands through her hair and rubbed her temples as she read the document lying on her desk. She hadn't slept well and had come in early, worried about her residents and how they were coping with the latest setback. She hoped they were doing better than she was. Things were remarkably quiet, with only the faint hum from the emergency lighting placed at intervals along the ceiling. The corridors were empty of anything other than mobility scooters and the ornaments and knick-knacks that most people put outside their doors to personalise their home. She looked at her watch; it was only just after half past eight – none of them got up particularly early and it took most of them a long while to get going in the morning.

She started to open the morning's post and then looked up, surprised, as the door opened. Most people who visited her office knocked before coming in. A vaguely familiar-looking man, followed by two very unfamiliar-looking thugs, strode in as if he owned the place. Lydia frowned at the interruption. 'Can I help you, Mr…?'

'Mahoney, hen.'

Of course, that's where she'd seen him before. A thoroughly unpleasant man. 'Ah yes. You were here with—'

'Fergus. Aye. Have you seen him?'

Lydia shook her head. 'Mr Lamont? No, why would I have seen him? He's stayed away ever since he decided to steal this place from our residents.' Her voice was sharp, and she was glad; she was fed up with being nice. She resolved to say exactly what she felt more often, especially to arrogant men like this one. She got up from her desk and went to the large window in her office that faced onto the corridor, and pulled the blind all the way up. She felt uncomfortable with these three in her office; at least with the blind up, anyone who passed would be able to see they were there. As she adjusted the strings to keep the blind raised, Sylvia's grandson Jake walked past, his motorbike helmet in hand. He glanced to the window, no doubt catching the movement in his peripheral vision, and gave her a cheery wave. Lydia responded with a smile and a wave back. Jake glanced curiously at the men in her office but carried on walking up the corridor to Sylvia's flat.

Lydia returned to her desk and sat down, realising that this put her in the inferior position to Mahoney, who was standing at the other side of the desk. Regardless, she didn't ask him to sit down; he probably wouldn't have anyway. A man like him clearly relished demonstrating his power over others. As if to prove her right, Mahoney stepped forward and planted his hands firmly on the desk, his face with its puckered scar looming over her. Clearly, he meant his move to be intimidating, and despite herself Lydia leaned back in her chair as far as she could.

'It's just business, Miss Wheelan, that's all. Nothing personal.'

He'd done that when he was here before, Lydia recalled: called her 'Miss'. Another power move. 'It's Ms. And I'm afraid that it *is* personal, Mr Mahoney. For the people who live here, of course it is. This is their *home*. So, no, I haven't seen Fergus Lamont, and quite frankly, I'd be happy if I never saw him again.'

Mahoney gazed at her for half a minute. He was clearly trying to scare her, and Lydia kept her lips firmly glued together. She gazed evenly back at him, her anger on behalf of the residents winning out over her unease at the presence of Mahoney and his thugs. Mahoney finally opened his mouth to speak, but before he could, there was a knock at the office door. Without taking her eyes off Mahoney, Lydia called out a tremulous 'Come in', extremely glad of the interruption.

The door opened and two police officers walked in. They took in the scene in the office and remained just inside the doorway. One of them looked at Mahoney and frowned, then turned to Lydia. 'Sorry to interrupt, Ms Wheelan, we just need a quick word.' The policeman looked curiously at Mahoney once again, as if he knew who he was.

Mahoney suddenly looked on edge and Lydia relaxed. He started to back away from the desk, and his two thugs sidled around the police officers and slid out of the door. The policeman who had spoken stepped in front of the door, blocking Mahoney from following them. 'I'm sorry, sir. I do hope I'm not interrupting anything?'

Mahoney smiled a cold, hard smile. 'No problem, officer. We were just leaving.' He took another step forward but the policeman didn't move.

The policeman took his eyes from Mahoney's for a moment to glance over at Lydia. 'Everything alright, Ms Wheelan?'

Lydia gave a brief nod. 'I believe so, officer. As Mr Mahoney said…' she stressed the name purposefully, to help the policeman out, 'he and his… associates were just leaving. What can I do for you, officers?'

The police officer looked for a final time at Mahoney and then stepped aside, before addressing Lydia. 'I'm Sergeant McGinlay and this is my colleague, Constable Hayden. We're wondering if you could help us. We're looking for a Mr Fergus Lamont.'

Mahoney stopped in the doorway. Lydia glanced at his rigid back and then returned her gaze to Sergeant McGinlay. 'You too?'

McGinlay hesitated a moment, as if confused, and then continued. 'Mr Lamont's secretary reported him missing. She says that the last time she saw him, she'd just taken a call from a…' He fished a notebook out of his pocket and laboriously leafed his way through it. '…a Mrs Sylvia Abercrombie.' He glanced around at a sound behind him and saw Mahoney still standing there. As he did so, Mahoney stepped out of the door, closing it behind him.

Sylvia's was the last name Lydia was expecting to hear. 'Sylvia?'

'Yes, ma'am, Sylvia Abercrombie. Mr Lamont's secretary said the woman sounded…' He read from the notebook again. '…as mad as a box of frogs.'

Lydia shook her head. 'There's no reason why *Sylvia* would contact Fergus Lamont, I'm sure. I don't believe she's ever spoken to him before; she'd have no reason to. His parents live here; are you sure it wasn't his mother, Ailsa?'

'No, it was definitely Sylvia Abercrombie, but we would like to speak to Mr Lamont's parents, too, while we're here. We'll do that first, I think.'

Lydia frowned. 'Of course, that would be sensible, as they're most likely to know, although he doesn't visit them very often, so…' She shrugged. 'But I can assure you that Sylvia *definitely* won't know where he is.'

'If it's all the same with you, we'll have a brief chat with her if we may, just to make sure she hasn't seen him. We wanted to check with you first; I'm sure that with the infirmities of the people in this Home—'

Lydia stiffened. 'It's not a Home, Sergeant. It's a retirement community.'

'I apologise. Retirement community, yes. We don't want to cause anyone undue alarm and distress, so we'd be more than happy if you wanted to accompany us to see Mr Lamont's parents, or Mrs Abercrombie. It's just a wee chat, I promise.'

Lydia bit back the grin that was forming on her face. 'I think Sylvia will be just fine without me being there, Sergeant McGinlay. She may be in a wheelchair, but she's definitely not infirm, as you alluded to earlier. And you can go and see Thomas and Ailsa yourselves, too. Sylvia's is number 3, the teal door. And Thomas and Ailsa are number 26. It's pink, with a statue of Eros outside. It's early for them, though, they'll probably still be in bed. Good luck getting them up.'

37

'WELL, THIS ISN'T AWKWARD AT ALL, IS it?' Sylvia pulled her thick cardigan more tightly around herself, over her winceyette nightie. Gregor and Jake were silently drinking cups of tea on opposite sides of the room. Gregor looked sheepish in his dressing gown and slippers, and slightly helpless without his teeth. He was staring fixedly at the floor and being of absolutely no help. Jake looked at each of them in turn, clearly baffled by the scene in front of him. His eyes rested on the obvious signs of Gregor's occupation in the flat – trousers flung over the back of the sofa, false teeth in a glass, his current get-up.

Jake turned to Sylvia with a hurt look on his face. 'Why didn't you tell Dad and me you two were back together?'

'It's no' like that, Jake.'

Jake looked pointedly at them both, and when he spoke his voice was sharp. 'Is it no'? You two don't speak for years and then I turn up unexpectedly and find you like…' he waved an arm at them, '… like this.'

Gregor sighed. 'Look, your gran's right. It's really no' like that, Jake. I wouldnae… I couldnae… I'm only here…' He lapsed into silence and looked at the two of them staring at him. He shrugged. 'If your gran hadn't got me into this mess…'

Jake shook his head. 'Yes, but *what* mess? You keep mentioning a mess and I don't understand what it is. The pair of you just clam up. Is one of you ill, or something? You *need* to tell me what's going on.' He sighed in frustration. 'All I see is the pair of you all cosied up like this. What am I *supposed* to think?'

Gregor slammed his cup down onto its saucer. 'Look – you think I *want* to be here? God, this is the *last* place I want to be, and *she's* the last person I want to be sitting here in my slippers with.'

Sylvia gasped and tried to hide her hurt. 'Aye, well, I'm sorry I asked, okay.' She turned her wheelchair away quickly, so that Gregor and Jake wouldn't be able to see the tears she felt stinging her eyes. 'Excuse me. I just need to… I'll go and…' She let out a shaky breath and then turned to Jake. 'Look, I'll just take a wee break, and when I come back, I'll explain everything to you, Jakey. It's all my fault and…' She started to wheel herself to the door, refusing to look at Gregor. A pain she hadn't felt for years settled itself in her throat and chest, tight and heavy. 'There's no need for you to be here when I get back, Gregor. I can manage on my own. Sorry to have bothered you.'

Sylvia closed the door behind her as she left the flat, and put her head in her hands for a moment to try to pull herself together. She would go and see Harriet; she'd listen to her and understand. But as she wheeled herself along the corridor towards Harriet's door, she spotted two policemen coming down the hallway towards her. She froze and then carried on slowly. They'd obviously been somewhere else in the building, so this was surely some sort of coincidence; it was simply that she felt guilty.

When the two officers saw her, they started to walk more quickly. 'Oh shite.' She swiftly turned her wheelchair and sped off in the opposite direction, back past her own flat and heading for the front doors. She could hear the two policemen breaking into a run behind her.

As they reached her, one of them knelt down in front of her, panting slightly, but smiling kindly. 'Mrs Abercrombie, isn't it?'

'No comment. And I'm neither deaf nor stupid, young man, so there's no need to shout at me like that.' She wheeled around to take off in the other direction again, but the second policeman was standing directly behind her. She ran her wheelchair over his foot, and he winced and hopped around in pain.

The first policeman bent down in front of her once more and put a hand on the arm of her chair. He said gently, 'My name's Sergeant McGinlay, Mrs Abercrombie, and I'm a policeman; we're looking for a Mr Fergus Lamont. You know who that is, don't you?'

Patronising git. She bit back the retort she wanted to make; his attitude was something which she was happy to use to her advantage. 'Who? What? I haven't seen him – never even heard of the man. No idea what you're talking about.' She manoeuvred herself around the two police officers. 'Now, if you two pig… errrr… nice polismen… would get out of my way, I have things to do.'

McGinlay put his hand more firmly on the arm of Sylvia's wheelchair, holding onto it so that she couldn't escape. 'We'd just like to ask you a couple of questions, Mrs Abercrombie. Could we, perhaps, step inside your flat?' He motioned his head towards the door they were standing in front of. 'It's this one, isn't it? My constable here could make you a wee cup of tea and we can get you settled comfortably.'

The big, assuming arsehole. Step inside her flat? God no. She needed to warn Gregor and Jake. 'My flat? You polismen want to go inside my flat?' The two policemen flinched at the sudden loudness of her voice. 'Intimidation! This is kettling! Police brutality! POLICE!'

Keys turned in doors, as the other residents reacted to the screeching outside by locking themselves in.

38

Jake had not entirely understood the tale his grandfather had told him, and the words 'spontaneous', 'hostage' and 'rubber' were now swirling around in his head. To try to clarify the situation, Gregor had taken Jake into Sylvia's spare bedroom and the pair of them were now standing just inside the doorway. The sight that met Jake's eyes wasn't helping. He was now even more confused. The room was dim; the curtains were drawn over the patio doors, with only a thin strip of light visible through the gap, filtered further by the net curtain. Jake looked from his grandfather to the bed in horror, finally deciding to focus on the bed where, lying on a bright and cheery handmade patchwork quilt in rainbow colours, was the rubber-clad, handcuffed form of a man, ball gag in mouth, squirming and writhing.

'He… looks a bit out of place, doesn't he?' Gregor sounded sheepish. 'On that quilt, I mean.'

Jake drew his eyes reluctantly away from the figure on the bed and stared at his grandfather. 'I can't believe you did this.'

'It wisnae me, it was yer gran! She hit him over the head with a vase – I had nothing to do with it!'

'Well, you're the only one here at the moment, so you're in charge of telling me *exactly* what happened until she gets back. And don't worry, I'll be having words with her, too.'

As if on cue, Sylvia's panicked bellow came from outside the flat. 'Intimidation! This is kettling! Police brutality! POLICE! Help! Kettling! Polis! They want to take me into my FLAT where they'll beat me with a rubber hose. IN MY OWN FLAT!'

Gregor put a hand over his eyes. 'Oh shite.' Jake took a step towards the door and then turned back to his grandfather.

Abercrombie put a hand on Jake's arm. 'Whit the fuck are we gonnae do?'

The shouting outside continued. 'You're no' coming in. You cannae come INSIDE MY FLAT. You've no' got a warrant! I'm no' letting you in.'

Abercrombie's hand gripped Jake's arm even more tightly and they both looked at the writhing body on the bed.

39

Sergeant McGinlay made soothing gestures with his hands. 'It's alright, Mrs Abercrombie. There's no need to shout. We're not kettling you, and we don't have any rubber hoses with us.' He looked over at the constable and raised his eyebrows. He moved towards Sylvia and patted her arm, trying to calm her, then stepped around her towards her door. 'Now, why don't you just let us in and we can discuss this. It's just a few questions. We have reason to believe you were the last person to see Fergus Lamont and we just want to have a wee chat, that's all.'

'I don't know what you mean.' Her voice was still a screech. 'I don't know the man. I've never seen him.' It wasn't working; the policemen were standing their ground. Sergeant McGinlay nodded encouragingly at the door. She'd just have to hope that Gregor and Jake had heard her and had managed to hide Lamont under the bed or something. Still shouting, she announced, very slowly, 'Fine then, I hope you're ashamed of yourselves for hectoring a poor old woman in a wheelchair.' She glared at them, happy to see that the constable, at least, looked guilty. The sergeant just looked bemused. 'I'm letting you into my flat. Do you hear that? I'm letting you in since you're resorting to police brutality. But I can assure you, you won't find anyone here.' She hoped so, at least. Taking her time, she fiddled with her key in the lock of the unlocked door for as long as she possibly could and then slowly opened the door a crack, before crossing the threshold at a snail's pace. The two policemen squeezed in behind her. Sylvia wheeled herself up the corridor of her flat. The door of the spare bedroom was open. She hesitated and one of the policemen bumped into her from behind.

'Sorry, Mrs Abercrombie.' It was the constable. She'd already hit him with her chair several times. His legs would be bruised to buggery. Good.

Sylvia ignored him and peered inside the door of the spare room. The rubber-clad body had gone from the bed, leaving only a dent in the covers. Gregor and Jake were nowhere to be seen either, and the net curtain over the now open patio door was billowing gently in the wind. Sylvia realised that she'd been holding her breath. She grinned and turned to the two policemen. 'Awright then, you lovely boys. Fancy a cuppa?' Her voice was now back to its normal level and the two officers appeared shocked by the sudden turn in Sylvia's tone of voice and demeanour. The second policeman made a twirling-finger movement at his temple. Sylvia pretended not to notice.

40

GRINDER HAD RETURNED TO HIS OFFICE AFTER the visit to Janus Lodge, and was now concentrating on the document in front of him. The pen moved very slowly in his hand as his frown deepened. PJ and Declan were standing at the other side of the desk, unsure as to whether they should sit down or not. He'd already bitten their heads off once for daring to interrupt him; they weren't about to do it again. They'd watched Grinder writing something painstakingly on pieces of paper for the last half hour, and then discarding the pieces of paper with a grunt. The desk and floor were littered with the results.

Finally, Grinder sat back in his chair and held up a piece of paper, putting his head on one side to stare at it for a moment. PJ took his chance. 'Boss?' His voice was tentative.

'Mmhmm?' Grinder's gaze remained fixed on the piece of paper.

'Whit are we gonnae dae?'

'About what?' Grinder's voice was absent-minded.

PJ glanced at Declan, who shrugged his shoulders. The effort made his breathing even more laboured. 'About finding Lamont, boss. We need to speak to that Abercrombie woman, don't we?'

Grinder put the document carefully back on his desk and crossed his arms. 'All in good time, PJ, all in good time. I don't think that's advisable right now, do you? The polis are all over that place looking for him. We don't want to draw attention to ourselves by going over there and harassing an old biddy, do we? That Wheelan woman is already suspicious of us. Besides, if the polis can do our job for us and find out where Lamont is, then so much the better.'

PJ blinked. 'But… whit about the deed thing you said he needed to sign?'

Grinder smiled. 'There's more than one way to skin a cat.' He picked up the document from his desk again and held it out. 'Here. What do you think?'

PJ leaned over to take a look, at first unsure of what he was seeing, but then light dawned. 'Is it the sale thing? For the property?'

Grinder dipped his head. 'It is indeed.'

PJ frowned. 'And Lamont's signed it?'

Grinder nodded once more. 'Indeed he has.' He pointed to a signature.

'But… when?'

Grinder placed the piece of paper back on his desk and tapped Fergus Lamont's flamboyant signature at the bottom. 'As I said, PJ; there's more than one way to skin a cat.'

As PJ looked on, confused, Declan lumbered over and placed a meaty hand on the desk. Grinder moved the paper away from him. Declan's fingers were always covered in grease. Declan frowned down at the document as if the act pained him. 'That's no' that wee nyaff's signature, is it, boss? He couldnae have signed it, 'cos he's vanished.'

'Indeed it is not, Declan, and indeed he *could* not. Well observed. But the main thing is that it looks like it. And it most definitely does, I'm sure you'll agree.' He pointed to another signed document at the front of the desk.

Declan was still leaning over the desk, frowning, looking from one piece of paper to the other. 'Aye, I wouldnae be able to tell the difference. But what is it, though, the document?'

Grinder carefully folded the signed document and put it into an envelope. 'This, Declan, is the final nail in the coffin of those old yins. This is an… entirely legal, by the way…' He hesitated a moment, grinning at his own cleverness. 'Well, *almost* entirely legal… document, drawn up by a *very* clever lawyer, which states that unless they can raise another two hundred and fifty grand by the end of the month, then Janus Lodge is mine.' He gazed from Declan to PJ and back again.

PJ wasn't entirely sure he understood what was going on and risked a question. 'But they *could* do it, couldn't they, boss? After all, they raised all that money before.'

'Aye, true enough, PJ, so they did. But they're not going to do it this time. They sold their little business to raise the last of the money they needed, and there's no way they'll be able to raise a quarter of a million in that time, no matter how hard they knit.' He wrote a name and address on the front of the envelope. 'Now, let's get this letter over to the lawyers so that they can deliver it to Janus Lodge on our behalf – I think it's best if we don't do that ourselves. And then we can come up with a plan for robbing our own bookies. I know you two have been looking forward to that.'

PJ's face brightened. 'When are we gonnae do that, boss?'

Grinder surveyed his manicured hands. 'All in good time, PJ. We'll give it a couple of weeks. By that time, hopefully, Lamont's whereabouts will have become clear.'

PJ's face fell. 'But what about him, boss?'

'Oh, I'm sure he'll turn up like a bad penny. I'm not overly worried; none of our businesses are missing any money, so it's not as though he's absconded with our takings or anything.' He barked out a humourless laugh. 'He's stupid, but he's not *that* stupid. We'll let the polis chase around at that old people's home – they won't get anything from those senile old fogies. Fergus is probably shacked up somewhere with his latest side piece. His absence could be a good thing for us, confuse the issue and all that. And if he's not turned up by the time we're ready to rob the bookies, we'll go and chat up that Abercrombie woman, just to cover all bases.'

41

Sylvia accompanied the two policemen down the corridor to the main doors of Janus Lodge, chatting happily as they went. 'Glad we got all that sorted out, lads. It was nice to chat wi' ye both. No hard feelings on the shins there, I hope, Constable?'

He shook his head in a bemused fashion. 'Naw, Mrs Abercrombie. Sorry I kept bumping into your wheelchair like that.'

'Aye, bit clumsy of you but it's fine.' She turned to McGinlay. 'An' Sergeant, next time you make me a wee cuppa, I'll thank you not to put any sugar in it. I near spat it out all over that nice jacket of yours, and then you'd have been draggin' me off to the cells, eh?'

'I'm sure we—'

'Anyway, I'll forgive you for that, an' for almost giving me a heart attack when yis came at me kettlin' me like that.'

'But we—'

'An' I hope you find that Lamont prick soon. He's an arsehole but his maw and da would miss him… well, they might not miss him, but I'm sure they wouldn't like to think of him lost, or dead, or trussed up like a kipper in a basement somewhere.'

'We can't—'

'An' I'm sorry you had to see the pair of them like that when Lydia took you along to see them. She should have realised that at this time in the mornin' they'd still be in bed an'… well… you saw their antics.' The constable let out a muffled sob. 'I'd like to have seen that, but you described the scene so well, Constable, it was almost like bein' there. Sorry if it put you off the wee bacon roll you were lookin' forward to back at the station, son. Anyway, I'm sure they were quite convincin' weren't they? It's difficult to lie well when you're in your naked strip an' clutchin' one o' they vibratin' rabbit things, isn't it?' It was McGinlay's turn to let out a pained whimper. 'Quite. Well, I'm sure you'll no need to be botherin' us again, scaring us all like that.'

They had reached the front door of the Lodge and Sylvia pressed the big button that opened the doors. 'Mind how you go then, lads. An' remember what I said about that new Public Order Act your lot have brought in. It's a pile of nonsense; see if you can get it changed. If I want to lock-on, I'll lock-on. If I want to carry a set of handcuffs with me at all times, it's up to me how I conduct my private life. I'm quite within my rights to protest, an' I'll be continuin' to do so when my conscience calls upon me to, right?'

'Aye but we—'

'Well, it was nice to have that wee chat, and I hope you can make your Chief Constable see sense on the matter. It's shocking how our rights are being taken away from us like this; it's bully boy tactics an' that never ends well. Right, see yous.' The door closed on the two policemen and Sylvia gave them a friendly wave. They hesitated a moment, then got into their car. Sylvia waited as they backed it out of the parking space before turning a beaming smile on them and waving to them once more. 'Aye, that's it, ya wee fannies, fuck off and don't come back.'

She watched as the police car drove slowly down the drive until she couldn't see it anymore and then knocked on Lydia's door. She waited for a response, then opened the door but didn't go in. 'Alright, hen?'

Lydia, a pile of papers on her desk, smiled at her. 'I'm good, you okay? Did the police come and see you?'

'Aye, they did that. An' they told me about goin' up to see Thomas and Ailsa, too. Did you do that on purpose?'

Lydia laughed. 'I did warn them. Well, sort of.'

Sylvia grinned. 'Aye, bit of a shock that, for those two nice young polismen. Catching Thomas and Ailsa *in flagrante delicto*, as they say. I think that sergeant was all for arresting them on the spot.' She thought for a moment. 'The G Spot, mibbee.'

Lydia ran her hands through her hair. 'Sylvia, you're incorrigible. Oh well, I'm sure they've seen worse.'

Sylvia gazed off into the distance. 'Actually, I'm not sure they will have, to be honest, love. It sounds like it was quite the sight; I feel a bit nauseous just from hearing about it. They had to have several cups of tea at mine to settle the nerves.'

'Oh dear. And had Ailsa and Thomas seen their son recently, do you know?'

'Not for weeks.'

'And you? Did you see him?'

Sylvia batted her eyes, the picture of innocence. 'Me? Naw. I haven't a clue where he is.' It was true. She didn't know where he was.

Lydia levelled a suspicious gaze on her. 'Why would they think you'd know, anyway? They said his secretary said there was a phone call?'

Sylvia shrugged. 'Beats me, hen… Anyway, you okay? You look tired. Pale.'

Lydia put her hands to her cheeks and gave them a rub. 'Oh, you know; just all this getting to me. Every time I think we'll be okay, something else happens and we're back where we started.'

'Well, don't you worry about it, hen. I've got a feeling everything will work out just fine.'

Lydia sighed. 'I hope you're right.'

'I am.' Sylvia backed out of the office. 'You should go home and get some rest. We'll be fine, all of us.' She took herself slowly back up the corridor, stopping at Gregor's door. Before she knocked, she glanced up and down the corridor. Nobody was about. They would need to be a bit more careful from now on; if people started gossiping, seeing them in each other's company after all this time, then they'd be drawing attention to themselves. She already felt guilty about dragging Gregor into this, and she didn't want him having to put up with awkward questions about whether they were getting back together. She sighed. That's if he was still talking to her; his words had shocked her, she really shouldn't have involved him like this. And then there was Jake; she'd dragged *him* into this too, now, and needed to make sure he wasn't affected. After all, it didn't matter to her – nobody was going to put a woman in her eighties in prison. Besides, she could simply plead insanity. There were plenty of people who would testify to that.

She gave a coded knock on Gregor's door, not that it would do any good, as she hadn't actually shared that code with anybody, let alone Gregor. The door opened a crack and Gregor peered out. His face mostly lost the worried look when he saw it was her, but not entirely. 'Come in.' He grabbed at her chair and pulled it in, checking up and down the corridor as he did so. He stood in front of her chair and cleared his throat. 'I'm… I'm sorry. For what I said. I didn't mean it. I'm sorry… for all of it.'

Sylvia was silent for a moment. There was more in his apology than just the harsh words in her flat earlier, she knew. 'You've no need to be sorry, Gregor; it wasnae your fault.' There was more meaning in her words, too, and Gregor nodded slowly. 'Now, come on, we'd better go and face the music. I'm sure you've been getting a tongue-lashing from Jake.'

Jake sat in Gregor's uncomfortable living room, arms crossed and stony-faced. For once, he didn't respond with his usual beaming grin when Sylvia went over and kissed him. 'You two have got some explaining to do.'

42

Lydia's eyes were stinging and she closed them briefly. She might head off home a wee bit early, just as Sylvia had suggested. The residents didn't seem to quite understand the importance of the latest developments and that was probably a good thing; but at least things couldn't get any worse. She picked up her mug and took a swig, grimacing as the cold tea went down. Had it really been that long since she'd made it?

She jumped at the swift rapping on her door. 'Come in!' Her voice was sharper than she intended, and she prepared herself to apologise to whichever resident it was.

'Miss Wheelan?' The man was unknown to her.

'It's Ms.' The sinking feeling in the pit of her stomach told her who this man had been sent by.

'I have a letter for you.'

He held it out to her, but she didn't take it. 'I don't want it.'

The man looked confused. 'You have to take it.'

She sighed and took it from him but didn't open it. The man shrugged and left the office. Lydia looked at the envelope as it sat malevolently on her desk, daring her to open it. 'Fine.' She snatched it up and tore it open, scanning the contents with dawning horror.

Finally, she pressed the button on the intercom system which would take her voice into every flat. In better times, the system was used to remind residents of quizzes about to start, or a musical act about to arrive, or that the fire alarm was about to be tested. Recently, however, she knew that residents had started to dread the sound the system made in their flats as the connection opened. She tried to make her voice sound as calm and soothing as possible, but she couldn't help the catch in her throat. 'Would all residents who are able to, please come to the Community Room in fifteen minutes. That's the Community Room in fifteen minutes. Thank you.' The system clicked off and Lydia started to cry.

43

SYLVIA AND GREGOR WERE AMONG THE LAST people to reach the Community Room. Harriet and Francine were tucked away in one corner looking nervously around. Sylvia waved and made her way over to them, followed by Gregor. They had left Jake in Gregor's flat, guarding their hostage.

Harriet's fingers were busy worrying at the LOC-8-OR device in her hands. She must have been investigating its possibilities when the announcement had been made and brought it with her. Sylvia looked down at the other part of the device on her wrist. It was still there from the latest game of hide-and-seek she and Harriet had played. The strap had been fiddly to get on, and she hadn't been able to unclasp it and had forgotten all about it. She'd need to give it back at some point, but she'd worry about that later.

Harriet leaned over and whispered feverishly, 'What's been happening? Archie said you'd been shouting in the corridor about being kettled by the police.'

Sylvia sniffed. 'Oh, he did, did he? Nice of him to come out and help me.'

'Is it true?'

'Aye.' Sylvia looked around but the nearest residents were deep in their own conversations. Sylvia beckoned Harriet and Francine to come closer and she quickly filled them in on what had been happening, while Gregor glanced nervously around to make sure nobody was listening.

Francine shook her head disapprovingly. 'So now you've got Jake involved in all this?'

'He's fine. He understands. And Lamont will never see him, or hear his voice. Besides, it'll be good to have some muscle around. Lamont's far too heavy for us to keep lifting all the time. Gregor borrowed that hospital bed on wheels out of the store cupboard, and Jakey got him onto that, so he can stay there for the time being. It's easy to move the bed, really smooth. We're…' She hesitated, knowing that what she was about to say wasn't going to go down well with Francine. 'Well, we're all gonnae have to take turns at looking after him.'

'And what, exactly, do you mean by "looking after him"?' Francine's voice was frosty, as though she already knew the answer.

Sylvia cleared her throat. 'Well, with the polis sniffing around, we're going to have to keep him on the move. You and Harriet have both got spare rooms.' She hurried on as Francine's mouth opened. 'Jake'll come and help us move him every couple of days. If we each take two days each, that'll nearly take us up to next Friday. And I'll do the extra shift,' she said, magnanimously.

'And what about his…' Francine was at a loss for words for once, and Sylvia bit back a grin, '…his… personal requirements?'

'Sortin' him out for a pish and a shite, you mean?'

'Sylvia!'

'Sorry, Francine. Well, Gregor'll do that, won't he? We've got Lamont on that hospital bed now, so Gregor will be lovely and comfy under your fancy candlewick bedspread in that spare room of yours, won't he? They come as a pair, him and Lamont.'

Harriet's eyes were bright as she pushed her heavy glasses up her nose. 'This is so exciting!'

Francine glared at her. 'Harriet! There's a man trussed up like a sausage in Gregor's flat; the police are looking for him; he knows who we are; and we're all going to spend the rest of our lives in jail. What's so exciting about that?'

Harriet looked at her blankly. 'Well… all of it.'

'Look, we're not going to go to jail.' Sylvia wasn't quite so sure of that, but she managed to say it with conviction. 'All we need to do is keep him hostage until the end of next week, and by that time the sale will be off and we can let him go.'

'For goodness' sake, do you think it will be as easy as all that? You think he's going to be happy when we'll have kept him encased in rubber for over a week, moved him around from pillar to post, and he's lost the money from the sale of the Lodge?'

Sylvia was triumphant. 'Ah, but he *hasn't* lost the money. *We're* buying the Lodge from him. We just want to keep him long enough so that he can't sign the document; that way, the sale to this Mahoney will fall through and *we* can buy it.'

'For less money than Mahoney's prepared to pay, according to our captive.'

Sylvia waved off Francine's objections, but was pleased that she'd called him *our captive*. 'It'll be fine. He'll be so relieved to be let out of that thing and have a guaranteed sale that he'll be thanking us.'

Francine scoffed. 'Thanking us? He'll have us all arrested.' The group's whispering was starting to get louder and more animated, and the other residents were looking at them in puzzlement now.

Sylvia lowered her voice again. 'Look, we'll just be really, really nice to him, give him a chance to air his grievances, sympathise, convince him that we're right… all that stuff. Who knows, maybe he'll get that Swedish thing.'

Harriet screwed up her face in puzzlement. 'Swedish thing?'

'Aye, that Swedish thing, that disease that they get in Oslo. You know the one I mean. Patty Hearst had it and it made her rob a bank.'

Francine and Harriet looked at each other. Francine groaned. 'Does she mean…?'

Harriet nodded. 'Yes, I rather think she does. Are you talking about Stockholm Syndrome?'

Sylvia beamed. 'Aye, that's the one. That Swedish disease. That's what I said.'

Francine opened her mouth to speak but at that moment Lydia clapped her hands at the front of the room. 'I'm sorry, everyone, but I have a bit of bad news. Two bits of bad news, really.'

The hubbub in the Community Room quieted and the residents gave Lydia their full attention. 'I'm very sorry, and I don't know how to phrase it so it's not a shock, so I'm just going to come out and say it. As you all know, we had a little bit bad news recently meaning that Lamont might not *have* to sell the place to us after all.'

Thomas Lamont spoke up. 'But you said our lawyers were looking into it.'

Lydia sighed. 'Yes, and they still are. But we've received something else just today.' Murmurs of distress went around the room. Lydia unfolded the letter in her hand. 'I'm afraid he's asking for another £250,000.'

The murmurs got louder. *Two hundred and fifty? Where are we going to get that? What are we going to do? We're going to be homeless.*

Lydia held up a hand. 'Look, it's not a lost cause. Look at all the money we raised before!'

Harriet raised a hand. 'But we've sold the business, and we included all the stock in the sale. We don't have the means of making money any longer.'

Lydia had already thought of this. 'With all the goodwill surrounding us and our story, we could start a GoFundMe; I'm sure we'd raise the money in no time.'

Half of the residents looked puzzled. The other half nodded sagely. It was clear to Sylvia who attended Tech Club. 'But it cannae happen anyway,' she said. 'This sale cannae happen until Fergus Lamont signs that document. And I understand he's gone missing, so he cannae sign it, can he?' Her voice was triumphant.

Lydia held up a hand as the residents started agreeing with Sylvia. 'Yes, well, apparently he's turned up.'

Sylvia, Harriet, Francine and Gregor looked at each other, horrified. 'Turned up?' Francine's voice quavered.

'Yes, he must have done. He's signed the document.'

'When?' Sylvia's voice was almost a growl.

Lydia looked at the bottom of one of the pieces of paper she was holding. 'Well… yesterday, I think. Yes. The document was signed yesterday.'

'But it can't have been signed yesterday; he's been—'

Francine jabbed Harriet in the ribs.

'Sorry, Harriet?' Harriet shook her head and Lydia continued. 'So, I'm afraid all this means that unless we can raise the additional two hundred and fifty thousand, then we won't be able to stay here. And even if we can raise that much… well… I don't know… we'll just have to wait and see if the lawyers come back with anything.' She looked around the room, clearly helpless. Residents were crying and consoling each other. She raised her voice. 'Please don't worry. We've still got hope. We'll set up that GoFundMe appeal and… and in the meantime, I'll start looking for places for all of you. Nice places, I promise. I won't let…'

As Lydia's voice caught in her throat, Sylvia turned to Francine, Harriet and Gregor. 'Come on, let's go to Harriet's and try to come up with a plan. Gregor, just nip in and let Jakey know we'll be a wee bit longer, will you?'

44

'HARRIET, YOU GET SAT DOWN AT MISSION Control and we'll do that brainstorming thing you're so fond of. Gregor, you can make us all a nice cup of tea while Harriet's getting set up with one o' they spreadsheet things.'

'What's the point?' His voice was defeated, but he obediently went into the kitchen anyway, returning in a few minutes with a tray of biscuits and sugar and a jug of milk, and then went back into the kitchen to wait for the kettle to boil.

Half an hour later, the spreadsheet was still blank and all of Harriet's biscuits had been eaten. Sylvia picked the last crumb off her plate. 'Well, this is bloody useless. We need to come up with *something*.'

Harriet sighed. 'Like what? We've done everything we can and it's still not enough. We're just going to have to face it – we'll have to leave our homes and I'll never see any of you ever again.' Her lip trembled. 'All I can hope is that the dementia comes on quickly and I won't even be aware of it.'

'Oh for fucksake, Harriet. Sorry, Francine. Don't get all dramatic on us – out of all of us, you're the one with a brain like a steel trap; you haven't got dementia. Who is it that wins all the quizzes and can remember who was in what film an' all that? It's not the rest of us, that's for sure.'

'But Harriet's right. There *isn't* anything we can do.' Francine was picking at a loose thread on the hem of her skirt so that she wouldn't have to look at the rest of them. 'Lamont and this Mahoney between them have got this all sewn up.'

'Aye, well, we're no' giving up. And remember, it might *seem* like the two of them have got it all sewn up, but we've got *Lamont* all sewn up and at the very least we can try to put pressure on him.'

Harriet snapped her fingers. 'Of course! We've got Lamont! We can just get someone to pay a ransom. How silly of us not to think of that straightaway. He's got to be worth two hundred and fifty thousand to someone! His wife, for one, surely?'

Sylvia snorted. 'Would *you* want to pay to get that wee shite back? Sorry, Francine.'

'I don't think we can.' Francine shook her head. 'That has to be a last resort, I think. Sylvia's already had a visit from the police because supposedly this was the last place he was seen; demanding a ransom would only draw the attention back onto us.'

'Aye, I'm not wanting to see they two polis again, I can tell you. We want them to think he's just buggered off somewhere. Sorry, Francine.'

Francine sighed. 'I think you can stop apologising to me every time you swear. After all, you've done far worse now, haven't you? I don't recall you apologising to me when you hit someone over the head with a Waterford Crystal vase and wrapped him up in rubber.'

'It wasn't Waterford Crystal. I bought it at the Barras in the 1970s.'

'Anyway, you're right.' Francine's voice was brisk. 'We *do* want the police to think he's just buggered off somewhere, as you so quaintly put it.'

Sylvia took a slurp of her tea. 'Exactly. Besides, who's going to want to pay the ransom? From what Ailsa says, his wife hates him; she's more likely to pay us to *keep* him. No, I think we need to work on him a little bit.'

Harriet turned pale. 'When you say "work on him"...'

Sylvia laughed. 'Not like that, hen. Look, he didn't sign that document that Lydia showed us; he was here all day yesterday. It must have been that double-crossing bastard Mahoney that did that. If we tell Lamont what he's done, then maybe we can persuade him to go along with us. He's our gambling chip in all this.'

'Gambling...' They all turned to look at Gregor.

Sylvia crossed her arms. 'Over my dead body. That was just one of the things that annoyed me about you when we were married.'

Gregor looked at her, a confused look spreading across his face. 'What?'

'You're no' gambling our hard-earned funds on the horses.'

'I wasn't going to—'

'*Or* the dogs.'

Gregor looked hurt. 'That's not what I was going to suggest.' He took his mug from the arm of the chair and placed it on the table, thinking. 'Look, we need money, right?'

Sylvia glared at him. 'Thank you, Captain Bleedin' Obvious.'

He ignored her and went on. 'And we'd like to get one over on Mahoney, right?' Francine and Harriet nodded; Sylvia continued to stare at him with her arms folded. Gregor ploughed on, realising that what he was about to suggest would pull them all deeper into the mire. 'Well, what if I've come up with a way we could solve both those things?'

'Go on.' Harriet moved her cursor into the first empty cell of the spreadsheet.

'No, don't write it down. I don't think it would be wise to have a record of this discussion.' Gregor sat back. 'And it will only work if we can get Fergus Lamont onside and get him to trust us.'

'And how do you suggest we do that?' Francine's voice was dubious. 'He's hardly going to be amenable. As we've already established, Sylvia hit him with a cheap vase and then we all had a hand in encasing him in rubber, and he's been in that situation ever since. It's hardly dignified for a man of his standing, is it?'

'Aye, well, maybe we can *start* with Sylvia's plan to turn him into Glasgow's answer to Patty Hearst and see how far that gets us.' Gregor smiled over at Sylvia and she realised it was the first smile he'd given her since their daughter died. 'We could call it… Operation Oslo. It sounds better than Stockholm.'

Harriet turned happily back to her computer screen and opened a Word document, typing in bold capitals along the top: 'OPERATION OSLO'. 'Don't worry, I'll write it in Chamicuro.' She turned away from the screen to find them all staring at her. ‘It was a southern Arawakan language previously spoken along the Pampa Hermosa River,’ she added, helpfully. It didn’t seem to help their understanding, so she said, ‘It’s a traditional ancient language of Peru. There are only about three people who speak it. Well, four if you include me.’

Sylvia laughed. ‘And you’re worried about going senile?’ She turned back to Gregor. ‘Is that the whole plan? Be nice to him until he can’t stand it any longer?’

Gregor shook his head. ‘Oh no, far from it. We need some information from him. That’s where we need to start.’

‘Information? What sort of information?’ Francine didn’t sound convinced.

‘I thought you’d never ask. Ladies…’ He looked at each of them in turn, his eyes sparkling. Sylvia hadn’t seen him like this in years, and a lump came to her throat. What a waste it had all been. ‘…we need the code for the safe.’

Harriet, who had been busily typing in what was, presumably, fluent Chamicuro, spun around in her chair. ‘Safe? What safe?’

‘The one at the bookies.’ The women looked at each other, confused, and Gregor patiently explained. ‘The bookies Lamont runs and Mahoney owns. The one I go to on Springfield Road.’

‘You mean…?’

‘Aye, Sylvie.’ He hadn’t called her that in years, and it pulled them both up short for a second. ‘We’re going to rob the bookies.’

There was silence for a moment as the three women tried to take in what Gregor had just said. Finally, Francine put her head in her hands and groaned. ‘What did I say about a last resort? Can we look at the ransom idea again?’

45

Over the last couple of days, the kidnappers had been all sweetness and light to their hostage, buttering him up in the hope that he might be more prepared to give them the safe code when they asked for it. Sylvia, Francine and Harriet had made sure the pillows on the hospital bed were plumped up, they'd baked him cakes and biscuits, and they'd even taken off his sensory deprivation mask from time to time. Sylvia had allowed him to listen to several episodes of *Judge Judy* and had kept up a running commentary of remarks detailing the absolute state of the defendants and plaintiffs in each of the cases. Harriet had shared her favourite philosophy podcast with him, and Francine had played him Elgar and Mahler to keep his spirits up. With Lamont strapped down to the hospital bed, he was easy to move from flat to flat, as they saw fit. They hadn't even needed Jake's help after Harriet had put WD40 on the joints of the bed, allowing it to roll even more smoothly and silently. Gregor and Francine were in charge of the moves, which happened at precisely two in the morning on moving days. He would be wheeled out of the patio doors of one flat, along the path outside, and in through the open patio doors of his next destination. Even the sills of the doors caused them no bother and the fact that they all lived on the same side of the building made the task easier.

While the three women were buttering up Lamont, Gregor, for his part, had haunted the bookies from opening until closing, carefully noting down – on betting slips which he made sure to take with him every day – the habits and routines of Agnes and the gormless young man, Aidan, who was the only other staff member. Gregor had discovered that he was Mahoney's nephew and that he was as useless as an inflatable dartboard. Gregor was there when they opened, and he was there when they locked up in the evening. Agnes and Aidan carried out the same locking-up procedure each day. Agnes watched over the lad as he checked all the doors every evening; she'd had to remind him several times to make sure the emergency exit at the back was firmly shut – it had a tendency to stick. Gregor filed that one away for future reference. He'd also noted that they never checked if there was anyone in the toilet, and that the alarm system sometimes didn't work properly. According to Agnes, who seemed to be enjoying Gregor hanging around and had become even more chatty than usual, Mahoney was too stingy to have the system fixed – which Agnes thought was a mistake, and Gregor privately agreed with her – so they didn't bother setting it any more.

Gregor had come up with a cautious plan and, as the day of the Old Firm game approached, his nervous excitement grew. In addition, his luck had been in – he'd had to make bets while he was in the bookies, of course, so that he didn't look suspicious, just lurking about – and he'd made a nice wee amount each day. Sylvia's Fancy had run yesterday and this time he'd happily placed a bet on it, and she'd romped home at a good price. He'd bought the actual Sylvia a box of chocolates with some of the proceeds but had been too nervous to give them to her, so had shared them with Lamont on his night-time hostage-sitting duties.

Today marked two days before the heist, and it was the day they had chosen to try to get the code out of Fergus Lamont. Gregor was unsure what they would do if he wouldn't give them the information.

He adjusted the hospital bed so that Lamont was sitting up and removed the sensory deprivation mask, but left the gimp mask in place. 'Morning, Fergus. Hope you slept well.'

An angry grunt was the only response. Gregor removed the ball gag and unzipped the gimp mask. 'When are you mad old fuckers going to let me go?' Lamont clearly wasn't in a good mood.

Gregor pulled a chair up to the side of the bed. 'Got some nice bacon and eggs for you this morning, Fergus. Your mum and dad told me it's your favourite.'

Lamont jerked back as far as his restraints and the tightness of the sleep sack would allow him. 'Are *they* in on this, too?'

'Oh, goodness me, no. Sylvia was just having a wee chat with them about you, is all, and that's one of the things that came up in their discussions.' Gregor picked up the plate and speared a piece of bacon on the fork. He put it to Lamont's lips. 'Here you go, nice and crispy.' It smelled delicious and Gregor's mouth watered. He'd get some for himself later. Lamont must also have thought it irresistible; after a moment's hesitation, he opened his mouth and Gregor steered the fork in. He couldn't resist: 'Choo choo!' and then felt a shaft of pain in his chest at the memory that came to him with the sound. He'd done it with Addy, his daughter, and with Jake when he was a baby; both of them had loved it. He cleared his throat. 'How are you doing today, Fergus?'

Lamont opened his mouth, and Gregor took the opportunity to fork in some of the creamy scrambled eggs. Lamont's voice was muffled. 'How the *fuck* do you think I'm doing? You're all in so much trouble when I get out of here.'

'And what do you intend on doing?' Gregor cut another piece of bacon and held it out on the fork.

Lamont automatically opened his mouth to accept the bacon. 'I'll get you all arrested, of course. What do you *think* I'm going to do?'

Gregor tutted. 'Now, I'm not sure you want to do that, Fergus. I don't think it would be at all wise.'

'What do you mean?' Lamont obediently ate the egg that he was offered.

Gregor silently fed him the rest of the plateful and then held out a mug. 'Coffee. Two sugars and some frothy milk. I've blown on it, so it's not too hot. It's that Italian hazelnut roast that's your favourite – another thing Thomas and Ailsa said you like. Harr— One of the team ground the beans for you.' Gregor could have kicked himself.

They'd purposefully not mentioned Harriet and Francine's names to Lamont, nor Jake's. The only voices he heard were those of Gregor and Sylvia, and the only name he knew was Sylvia's – it was pointless keeping her name a secret when she was the one who'd hit him over the head in the first place. 'You've got expensive tastes, haven't you?' Lamont took a sip and then another. 'Anyway, you were asking why it wouldn't be a good idea to go to the police.' He wiped some froth off Lamont's lip and sat back in his chair, his back aching from being crouched forward over the bed.

'Of course I'm going to the police.'

'Well, you see, that chat Sylvia had with your parents was very interesting. It wasn't all about your favourite things to eat and drink, you know.'

'What do you mean?' Lamont's voice had less bluster in it than before, as though he had guessed what Gregor meant.

'Well, you see, they told Sylv about some particularly fascinating business arrangements you have, ones which the polis would be *very* interested to hear about, I'm sure.'

'I don't know what—'

'No? I think you do. And not only the police, but I think the press would be all over this one. And your wife… well, Thomas and Ailsa aren't fond of *her*, are they? But the important fact is that *she's* not fond of *you*. This could all cost you a pretty penny if it gets out, Fergus, not to mention a good few years in jail.'

'But that's—'

'Now, you might end up in one of those fancy jails; you know, where you'd be surrounded by other fraudsters, embezzlers and insider traders… your own kind, so to speak, but I still don't think you'd like it. No, your parents were very chatty on the subject.'

'They're senile. Nobody will believe them.' The panic was evident in Lamont's voice now, and Gregor grinned to himself.

'Oh, don't worry. They've got the paperwork to back it up, according to Sylvia. That briefcase you gave them a couple of years ago? For safekeeping? Well, they gave it to Sylvia. For safekeeping. And she managed to… well… break into it. With a hairpin, of all things, just like you see in the films. *The Big Sleep* and *Kiss Me Deadly*, apparently. She loves a bit of film noir, does Sylvia.'

'No! I… You can't do that.' Lamont was clearly casting around for his options. 'I know people. Nasty people. If I can't go to the police, I'll go to them.'

'Like this Mahoney of yours?'

'Exactly!' Fergus's voice was triumphant. 'As soon as he finds out what you've done, he'll come looking for you. All of you.'

'You think?'

'I know!'

'Hmmmmmm, I'm not so sure of that.' Gregor collected the plate, mug and cutlery, and took them into the kitchen. When he returned, he eased himself back into his chair with a groan. 'Do you think this Mahoney character cares about you? Do you think he'd, say, pay a ransom?'

'Ransom? Is that what this is all about? Is that why you mad old bastards kidnapped me, for money?'

'Actually, no, it wasn't. You told Sylvia that if you didn't sign the document for the sale before this coming Friday, then the deal would be off.'

Lamont laughed with relief. 'So that's it? You'll let me go after that?' The relief was short-lived, however, as he clearly remembered an obstacle. 'But then… I'll owe Grinder for breach of contract.'

'Well, you can sell the place to us, as agreed, and then you can just pay him back.'

'But that won't get me *all* the money back. Grinder has… Besides, Grinder really wants this site and he needs me to sign this document. He'll pay any ransom you ask. And he'll pay *you* all back, too.' Lamont shivered in his sleeping sack, like the fat little slug he was, Gregor thought. 'I wouldn't want to be in your shoes.'

Gregor leaned forward. 'I don't think Grinder needs you quite as much as you think, Fergus.'

Lamont stopped wriggling. 'What do you mean?'

'Well, that document he needs you to sign? It's already been signed.'

'Signed? By who?'

'By you. Two days ago.'

Lamont's head reared back as far as it could go, given the restriction on his movements. 'Two days ago? But I was…'

Gregor patted his shoulder. 'Exactly, Fergus. That's exactly it. And, while that doesn't mean he can get the Lodge on that basis alone, the document also says if we want to buy it then we need to come up with another £250,000. And we only have the rest of the month to do so. After that, it seems as though he's free and clear, thanks to this fake signature. You see, he doesn't need you, after all, and he's not going to blaze in here on a white horse to rescue you any time soon.'

'Oh my God.' Lamont's voice was frantic now and he was hyperventilating. Gregor put his hand more firmly on Lamont's shoulder, to try to calm him. 'Look, what do you want? Why are you doing this to me?' His voice was pathetic.

This was the moment to get the code. 'You know what we want, Fergus. We want our home to remain our home, and only you can do that for us.'

'But how? You just told me…'

Gregor leaned forward and put his mouth to Lamont's rubber-covered ear. 'We need the code for the safe at the Springfield Road bookies.'

'What?' It came out as a squeal.

Gregor crossed his fingers and kept his voice calm. 'The code for the safe.'

'What… what are you going to do?'

Gregor laughed softly. 'I thought that would be obvious. We're going to rob it.'

Lamont whimpered. 'You can't… you can't. Mahoney will…' He broke off and his voice, when he spoke again, was firmer and contained an element of spite. 'He'll kill you. Besides, I'm not giving you the code.'

'No, he won't kill *us*, Fergus. If you don't give us the code then we'll have to use dynamite.' Gregor hoped Lamont didn't ask how they were going to get it or whether they knew how to use it, because he could answer neither of those questions. He hurried on. 'And we'll leak the information that the robbery is all down to the very missing Fergus Lamont.'

'Noooooo!'

'But if you *do* give us the code then that information won't be leaked at all. And nobody will ever know who was responsible. I can assure you, our team is made up of some highly professional and trained individuals and we'll be in and out smoothly, swiftly and silently.' Gregor was particularly proud of that speech. He'd been practising it in front of his bathroom mirror for the last two days. But his well-rehearsed words had fallen on deaf ears. Lamont was rocking from side to side, sobbing.

46

'SO WHEN ARE WE DOING THE JOB, boss?' PJ sniffed and wiped the back of his hand across his nose, glancing down briefly at the wetness left behind.

Grinder shuddered and made a mental note to wipe down everything in the office that PJ touched, once he had left. 'Day after tomorrow – takings will be good after the Old Firm match and Agnes won't pay them into the bank until the following day.' PJ nodded. 'Oh, and it's just you. I don't want Declan in there rampaging about like a bull in a china shop; you won't need the muscle – it'll just be a quick in-and-out. You'll have the key to the back door, the alarm code and the safe code. I want you in there at three o'clock in the morning, and out by half past. Don't bother resetting the alarm when you leave, and leave the safe door open and the back door unlocked. We can blame this on Agnes; she's been moaning on about us letting go of Big Stevie and having to babysit my idiot nephew. With Lamont doing his disappearing act, I'm fed up of having to deal with her.'

PJ nodded. 'It'll be a piece of pish. No worries, boss.'

'It's the most straightforward job in the world. Nothing could possibly go wrong. Just remember to wear gloves and bring me that spare key back the next day.'

47

SYLVIA HAD PARTIALLY RELEASED LAMONT FROM THE rubber sleeping bag after he'd complained about being too hot. His skin was red and sweating, and it looked as though he'd taken an allergic reaction to the rubber. Gregor had helped her to tie Lamont even more firmly to the hospital bed, and she'd put the back of the bed up straight so he could sit up. Gregor had helped her to give him a sponge bath and put a clean, fresh T-shirt on him, and Lamont was now sitting with the top half of his body free of the bag. The gimp mask was still in place and the zip was firmly closed, but he could hear and, if he wanted to communicate, he was able to sound out muffled words under the mask, which she was getting good at deciphering.

Sylvia was sitting by the bed, struggling with a huge heap of tangled yarn – most of it Nettie's baby-blue wool. 'Here, you can make yourself useful while you're just lying there. Hold out your arms… no, not like that, just in front of you, as if you were a zombie in a film… That's it.' She started to wind the wool into a hank, around his arms. 'There, that's perfect. An' while we're doing this, you an' me can have a nice wee chat, can't we?' She drew her chair up closer so that she could still reach Lamont's arms and settled back more comfortably, winding expertly. 'Now, I understand that you weren't very polite to one of my colleagues, when all he was askin' for was just a wee bit of information.'

Lamont made noises behind the mask. 'Ooh, Fergus, that's no' very nice either, is it? You do understand that we're the ones holdin' all the cards here, don't you? I don't think calling me a "mad old bag" is a particularly good idea.' Lamont dropped his arms and struggled against the straps that bound him to the bed, grunting noisily. 'Now look what you've done. We'll have to start that hank again, an' we were doing so well.'

She frowned as she started off the hank again. 'We've tried kindness, but you throw that back in our faces; we've threatened you with the polis and with exposure of all your wee schemes to the newspapers; we've told you about your sleazy pal Mahoney doin' the dirty on you. I'm not sure what else we can do.'

She paused in her winding to listen closely to Lamont's frantic but indistinct mumblings. 'No, Fergus, just lettin' you go is *not* an option, I'm afraid. An' some of us are getting quite fed up of your obstreperousness. There has been talk of violence.' Lamont's mumblings faded to a low panting and his body stilled. 'There, that's much better when you keep your arms still like that. Good lad.' Sylvia wound the yarn a few more times in silence before continuing in conversational tones. 'We thought a bit of psychological torture might be good. Music was discussed as an option, but we couldn't agree on what type. Some of them wanted to use my thrash metal collection, but I thought that would be wasted on you. I asked your maw and da if you were afraid of spiders or anything, so that we could introduce those, but they didn't think you had any phobias.'

Lamont tried to speak once more and Sylvia grinned. 'Aye, good one, Fergus. No phobias apart from being kidnapped by senile old codgers, then. One of our number introduced us to a new concept: *bastinado*. Any idea what that is?' Sylvia had been impressed at Francine's knowledge of Ancient Roman torture methods. 'It's having the soles of your bare feet whipped.' She paused, waiting for a response, but Lamont was silent. 'That person also suggested putting you in a sack with a dog, a snake, a monkey and a chicken and then throwing it into the water, but we all said no to that one, on the grounds of cruelty to the dog, the snake, the monkey and the chicken. Besides, it would be tough to get our hands on a monkey at such short notice. We don't have the time to nip up to Blair Drummond Safari Park, what wi' everything else that's going on.'

She took the first hank of yarn off Lamont's arms and started on another. 'I'm particularly attached to the idea of waterboarding, but it's got such a bad rep recently that the others voted me down.' She sighed. 'Oh well, I'm sure we'll come up with something eventually. It would be nice to know if you're scared of anything, so if you feel like sharing, please do.'

There was a staccato *tap-tap-tap* at the patio doors. The curtains were tightly closed against prying eyes, but the tap was their agreed signal and Sylvia wheeled her chair over, parting the curtains a fraction, before unlocking the door and sliding it to one side to let Francine in. She put a hand to her lips to remind her to be silent around Lamont, so Francine held up the bag of craft items she was carrying. 'Ooooh, thanks. Is that the extra-large crochet hooks I was looking for?'

Lamont started to thrash about on the bed and scream behind the mask.

48

THE FOUR CONSPIRATORS HAD GATHERED IN HARRIET'S flat and were celebrating with a bottle of sherry that had been in her kitchen cupboard since the previous Christmas. Francine raised her glass in a toast. 'To the power of crochet to reduce grown men to quivering wrecks.'

'Hear, hear, Madam Chairman!' Sylvia clinked her glass against each of theirs in turn. 'Who would have thought that all we needed to do all along was show him a crochet hook? I'm not sure what he thought we were going to do with it.' She paused thoughtfully. 'I'm almost sad that he gave the code up so easily after that; it would have been fun to find out.' Her tone was one of regret but then she snapped out of it. 'Ah well, you can't have everything. So, let's plan this heist. How are we going to do this?'

Gregor shook his head. 'There's no "we" involved. *I'm* doing this by myself.'

'You can't do that!' Francine's voice was stern. 'You can't take all that risk yourself.'

'And you need backup. I'll do it.' They all looked at Harriet as she struggled to get out of her chair.

'Sit down, hen.' Sylvia's voice was kindly but firm. 'Let's face it, none of us are going to be of any remote use. What Gregor needs is a… hatchet man in a bulletproof Cadillac.'

Francine looked at Sylvia over the top of her glasses. 'You've been watching too many of those late-night film noirs again.'

Sylvia flung out an arm. 'Made it, Francie! Top of the world!'

'You're ridiculous, dear.' Francine turned back to Gregor. 'You do need something – backup, a weapon?'

Gregor shook his head. 'Naw. I don't need anythin'. No weapons, no backup; they could cause more trouble than they're worth. Look, that place is askin' for it: they've got no security, lax procedures and there'll be a safe stuffed full of money that we have the code for. I'll hide in a wee cupboard that's tucked away in one of the toilets. I've checked it out an' it's big enough; I'll slip in at closing time. It'll be about ten o'clock because of the match an' the place will be heavin'. Then I'll give it a few hours – it'll be busy outside because of the pub next door. I thought about two o'clock I'd pop out of ma wee hidey-hole, unlock the safe, put the cash in my backpack an' let masel' out of the back door.'

'And how are you gonnae get home? You at least need a getaway car.'

Francine sighed. 'For a start, Sylvia, none of us has a car.'

'We could hire one. You drive.'

Francine shook her head. 'And that's not going to look at all suspicious, is it? I hire a car for the first and only time since I've been living here, drive it out of here in the early hours of the morning and sit outside the bookies waiting for a man to appear from the alley with a backpack full of cash.' She sighed. 'This is ridiculous. I don't even know why we're discussing it as a possibility.'

Gregor stood up. 'It's happening. It's a ten-minute walk home from the bookies at most. There's a wee path at the other end of the alleyway that goes to the back door of the bookies. I'll go that way. It's only slightly longer and the path is mostly covered by trees.'

Sylvia sat back, beaming. 'That's that, then. Sorted. I'll make you a nice wee sandwich for your wait in the cludgie.'

Francine was still unconvinced. 'And then what do we do with a sack full of cash? We can't exactly take it to the bank, can we?'

'Oh, that's easy.' Harriet spun her chair around to the computer screen and brought up the GoFundMe page she and Lydia had set up. There was already just over £50,000 in it from generous supporters, but the rate of donations had slowed in the last day. 'Bitcoin. I'll set up a cryptocurrency account and a Web3 username on Coinbase or Uniswap, so that we can use that instead of the wallet address. Those hexadecimal addresses are too cumbersome. It's as easy as that.' They were all looking at her, baffled. 'Then all I'll need to do is use GoFundMe's off-platform donation system to transfer the crypto.'

Sylvia spread her hands and looked at Francine and Gregor, who shook their heads. 'Me neither. Not a fuckin' scooby.'

'Oh for goodness' sake. You three need to get with the digital age. Basically, I'm going to set an anonymous payment which we can pretend comes from a shy billionaire donor.'

'Well, why didn't you just say that?' Sylvia frowned. 'But *are* there any shy billionaires? They all just seem to be loud-mouthed arseholes who need to be fired into space.'

49

GREGOR WAS IN HIS USUAL SPOT IN the bookies. He'd been there since six and the place was mobbed. Agnes and the wee plooky lad, Aidan, had been struggling to cope all evening. The bets – and, therefore, the cash – had been flying in, both pre-game and in-play: the optimists betting on their team to win by a massive margin, the pessimists going for a dull nothing-each draw. Punters were betting on who the first player to score would be, who the last player to score would be, the score at half time, number of corners, number of red cards, penalties, man of the match, which player would take a shite in the away goal, what minute of the game an alien spaceship would land in the centre circle… the list was endless.

Stevie had been much missed this evening. He could always be relied on when there was an Old Firm match to knock a few heads together as temperatures were raised and rival supporters came to blows. The game had been end-to-end stuff and there'd been more than a few fisticuffs thrown this evening. Agnes had waded into the fray on several occasions, but she'd given up towards the end and just let them get on with it. In the eighty-seventh minute, Celtic had scored the decider and all hell had broken loose. A rammy of massive proportions broke out and Gregor was worried that the police would be called, so he jumped off his stool and did his best to calm things down. Luckily, a couple of the other regulars did the same and the battle of the bookies was over almost as soon as it had begun.

Torn-up betting slips were flung like confetti as pissed-off punters took out their rage on pieces of paper at the final whistle. The few who had made correct guesses queued up to collect their winnings and everyone else started to drift away, to call in at the pub next door for a celebratory pint before closing time or to slink off home and lick their wounds. It was Gregor's chance to slip away to his cupboard in the nearest of the two toilets. He'd already visited it a few times, in order to clean out some of the items inside the cupboard and tuck them away elsewhere so that he could squeeze himself in. Luckily, the cupboard had been pretty empty – a grimy mop and bucket, some cleaning supplies and a few random items that had seemingly been left by forgetful gamblers over the years. Gregor had cleared out all but the mop and bucket; there was nowhere to put those without it looking obvious, and either Agnes or the lad might decide to tidy up and put them back where they belonged. He'd also held onto an old anorak he'd found in there, which he put on the floor of the cupboard to sit down on. Sylvia had given him some elastic, which he tied around the knobs inside the cupboard once he'd squeezed himself inside. Anyone casually trying the doors would assume they were locked. With some difficulty, he sat himself down on the anorak and settled in for a few hours' wait.

The sounds from the rest of the building gradually subsided and the dings that signified that the door of the bookies was opening and closing speeded up and then slowed down again as people left. Soon, all he could hear was Agnes's raised voice as she tore a strip off Aidan for some unspecified infraction, and then that, too, ceased.

The door of the toilet opened and Gregor held his breath. It was Aidan, grumbling away to himself under his breath. Gregor heard a long stream of urine hitting the pan and a sigh as the lad zipped up his jeans. He left the toilet – without washing his hands, Gregor noted – and went back out into the corridor.

Gregor looked at his watch. Eleven. The bar on the fire door at the back entrance clanged open. 'See ya, Agnes.' The lad left, slamming the door behind him. Gregor could hear Agnes in the front, presumably doing the last of her duties before finishing locking up. Surely she'd leave soon. Gregor couldn't wait to stretch his legs. He wouldn't leave the toilet area, but at least he could get out of this cupboard. He rubbed his knees. He was too old for this sort of thing.

As he sat and waited for the fire door to signify Agnes's departure, he wondered, not for the first time, how he'd got himself into this, and smiled wryly to himself. Sylvia, of course. They'd known each other since they were babies; their families had lived next door to one another, up a close in the Gorbals. They'd grown up together, their own mini gang, egging each other on into scrape after scrape. They'd been in the same class at school all the way through, and they still hadn't needed anyone else. Then they'd suddenly found themselves all grown up. Gregor had gone to work in the shipyards, Sylvia as a secretary at the local biscuit factory. And that's when their relationship changed, slowly but surely, into something else. Nights spent dancing at the Locarno, The Plaza, The Barrowlands, The Palais; Saturday afternoons at the Cosmo, The Astoria and the Lyceum watching his favourites – romances – and Sylvia's favourites – gangster thrillers. They'd gone on day trips to Ayr and Troon, and other places down the coast. They'd had so much money back then, it seemed to them, enjoying their new jobs and proud to pay their respective maws a wee fraction of their wages.

He'd realised, not long after they both turned eighteen, that he loved her, his Sylvie, but it had taken a year for him to pluck up the courage to tell her that. And when he had, she'd simply said, 'I know that, ya big daftie.' And that had been that. A lifetime of happiness lay in front of them. Gregor sighed and tears pricked at his eyes. It turned out that the happiness didn't last nearly long enough. He wouldn't think about those years; he nearly didn't survive them. Thoughts of doing away with himself had been there every day since. Every single day from the day of the accident until… until the day that Sylvia had dragged him into her flat to show him the crumpled body of the man on her living room floor. This last wee while he'd felt happier than a pig in shite. He'd missed her so much, but hadn't been able to bear looking at her in the hospital bed and then in the wheelchair that had been his fault. He'd missed his Sylvie, and he'd missed his grandson, and, he realised, he'd missed himself. And now here he was, folded uncomfortably into a stinking cupboard in the cludgie of a seedy bookies, and he couldn't have felt happier or more alive.

At last, the fire door slammed once more and there was nothing but silence. Gregor reached into the gym bag he'd brought for the cash and took out the sandwiches Sylvia had made him. He'd just have these while he waited to make sure that Agnes didn't come back, then he'd stretch his legs. He unwrapped the tinfoil and the scent of strong cheddar and Branston pickle hit his nose. He smiled; Sylvie had remembered his favourite.

He wolfed the sandwiches down – he hadn't realised quite how hungry he was – and then slowly and carefully stood up, holding on to the mop handle to help haul himself up. His knees creaked in dismay and Gregor groaned along with them. He removed the piece of elastic from the doorknobs and slowly opened the door and staggered out. It was dark in the small anteroom but he could just make out the wee sink on the other side of the space, and the open door of the toilet cubicle itself.

He bent and flexed his knees a few times and then tottered over to the door that led to the hallway by the fire door. He wouldn't go out quite yet, but he'd just open it a wee bit so that the greenish glow of the Emergency Exit sign would give him a bit more light. He put his hand on the handle of the door and turned. Nothing happened. He pulled the door towards him and turned the handle again. The door remained steadfastly closed. He'd been locked in.

50

PJ WAS PREPARING FOR HIS BIG NIGHT by watching *Despicable Me* for the ninety-sixth time. It was his favourite film and always calmed his brain. He looked at his watch. Still just over three hours until he had to leave. Grinder had made him promise: in at three o'clock, out by half past, and he was repeating it like a mantra to himself. He'd checked and double-checked that he had the key to the building and the alarm and safe codes. He'd dressed carefully for the occasion: black tracksuit, black trainers (he'd used a marker pen to cover up the bright white swoosh; he hoped he'd be able to wipe it off afterwards, they were his favourites), black jacket and black balaclava. He decided to take the balaclava off for a wee bit, while he watched the end of the film. He looked at his watch again. Still more than three hours until he needed to leave.

51

GREGOR DIDN'T THINK THAT THE KEY WAS in the keyhole, because he could see a faint green light when he peered through it, but it wouldn't have helped anyway. The door was tight to the floor. He'd tried slipping a sheet of the hand towel underneath, just in case, but he couldn't even slide the paper under.

There was nothing to be done. He'd be released the next morning when the bookies opened, and the best course of action was to pretend that he'd collapsed in the toilet the evening before and had accidentally been locked in. He ran a hand over his face, despondently. They'd never have such an opportunity again and he'd gone and spoiled it. He'd need to phone them: Sylvia, Francine and Harriet had said they would wait up for him at Francine's, where Lamont was tucked away in the spare bedroom. Gregor sighed. He'd let them down and he felt a sickness in the pit of his stomach. He hesitated a moment, but there was nothing else for it; he should get it over and done with as soon as he could. He reached into his pocket for the mobile phone he hardly used, and realised he'd left it in his flat.

52

FRANCINE LOOKED AT HER WATCH. 'THAT'S IT, I'm going to take a walk down and see where he is. That's half past two; he should have been here by now.'

'Calm yer jets, doll.' Sylvia raised a hand to stop her. 'He wasn't going to move from his wee hidey-hole until two. Then he'll have to open the safe and unload the cash into his bag. An' you heard him; he's going to come home the long way round.'

'He should be here by now,' Francine insisted. 'I'll give him another five minutes and that's that.' She stood up and paced the floor.

Sylvia looked at Harriet and shook her head. 'He'll be here, don't you worry. An' he won't want you goin' after him. You heard how adamant he was about that. My Gregor was always a determined man.'

Francine glanced at Harriet and raised her eyebrows at the *my Gregor.* Harriet smiled and put a finger to her lips. Francine checked her watch once more. 'Right, that's it.' She walked into the hallway and took her coat down from its peg.

Sylvia wheeled herself out into the hallway. 'We'll come with you, then.'

'You most certainly will *not.* You two aren't fit for it. I'll be quicker on my own.'

'Well, cheers for that.' Sylvia looked at Harriet. 'Bloody cheek of her.'

Francine buttoned up her coat and tucked one of her long, bright scarves about her ears and inside the collar of the coat. 'Besides, someone needs to stay with Fergus. I'm sure I won't be long.'

53

PJ PULLED UP AROUND THE CORNER FROM the bookies. He'd stolen a car from a sports centre car park just ten minutes before. Grinder had refused to let him drive the Mercedes and PJ hadn't wanted to walk. He was rather pleased with himself for his choice of car. The sports centre was shut, so nobody was likely to come out after a session in the gym looking for their car. Serve the owner right for leaving it in an unsecured car park like that.

He checked his watch. Ten minutes to three. This was the first time Grinder had trusted him to do a job on his own, and PJ was determined to do it by the book, exactly as Grinder had told him to. He smiled to himself. Dec had not been happy that PJ had been chosen over him, and it had taken all his willpower not to rub Dec's nose in it. PJ was Grinder's right-hand man; he felt it. He'd better think about buying a suit; trackies weren't the right look for a gangster's second-in-command.

At exactly one minute to three, PJ got out of the car, gently closed the door and walked around the corner to the bookies. The bookies, the pub next door, the chemist's shop and the two fast food places that made up the stretch of shops were all in pitch darkness. They were all single-storey, so there were no nosy neighbours living upstairs, and opposite them were the metal railings of a small park, one which was locked up at eight on the dot every evening. Two huge trees, PJ didn't know what sort, stood outside the park and their branches hung over the road, green and heavy. Unusually for this area, each of the shops was detached, with a narrow alleyway running in between each of them. The two fast food places kept enormous bins around the side that you could just squeeze past, but all the alleyways led to a narrow back road, parallel to the main one at the front of the shops.

PJ glanced around. Now he was here, his heart was pounding with a mixture of nerves and excitement, and he shook off the vague feeling that he was being watched. He pulled the key out of his pocket and walked into the alleyway at the side of the bookies, stepping carefully over the bottles and cans that had spilled out of the bin. With some difficulty because of the darkness, he put the key in the lock and turned it. The door creaked open and he stepped inside.

54

Francine stepped out from behind the tree she had ducked behind when she saw the interior light of a car parked just around the corner come on, and the driver's door open. A young man dressed in black had stepped out of it, walked up to the main road and gazed up at the row of shops. Perhaps a night worker hopefully looking for something hideous made from unmentionable bits of chicken. She shuddered at the thought. He would be out of luck, everything was shut.

She watched him as he hesitated at the top of the alley that led to the side door of the bookies and looked around. Francine held herself close to the tree, partly to make sure she wasn't seen, but partly to stop herself from falling over. The man disappeared out of sight and it was Francine's turn to hesitate. Who was this man, and why was he here? Was Gregor still inside? If not, then where was he? Something had clearly gone wrong, and Francine knew that she couldn't leave without knowing what it was. What if something had happened to Gregor?

Francine crossed the road and moved to the corner of the bookies. She peered around the corner into the alley. It was dark and quiet, but a thin sliver of light came from the side door, which was slightly ajar. The man must have gone inside. She tiptoed up to the door and put her eye to the crack. The young man was staring at an alarm panel on the wall, looking puzzled. Eventually he shrugged and turned away. Francine drew back and held her breath. As he had turned and the light had caught his face, she had recognised him. He was one of the men who'd accompanied Mahoney to Janus Lodge one day. She'd seen him, lounging by a fancy car while she was out tending to the plant pots on her patio. A surge of anger was replaced by a deeper sense of worry. What *had* happened to Gregor?

She peered through the gap in the door once more. There were three doors in the hallway. Two of them had toilet signs on them, the third was blank. The young man turned the handle of the plain door, but it appeared to be locked. As though he knew exactly what he was doing, the young man opened the door of a small cupboard set into the wall between that door and the first of the toilet doors, and took out a key. He put it in the keyhole and turned it, then hesitated. 'I need a pish,' he murmured to himself, and took another key out of the wall cupboard.

As he inserted it into the keyhole of the first toilet door, however, he stopped before turning it. 'What the fuck… Who's there?'

Francine had heard the noise too, a clattering coming from the other side of the door. 'Who's that?' came a voice from inside the toilet. *Gregor.* Francine knew she couldn't let this thug go in there and see Gregor. Not only might he do something to him, but if he saw him, then all their plans would be for naught. Without hesitation, she pulled her scarf from her neck and tied it around her face, covering everything but her eyes. She tucked the trailing ends back inside the collar of her coat and pushed the door open with a fierce cry.

The door slammed against the wall behind it and the thug turned round. Francine stepped inside and, launching herself forward, she raised her right hand across her body until it was level with her left ear, palm facing down. As she used her weight to propel herself towards the stunned young man, she swung the hand in an outside chop, the side of her hand connecting with his neck. He let out a gurgling scream, collapsing inwards on himself. Before he could fall to the floor, Francine followed up immediately with a palm heel strike to the base of his nose. She could almost hear his brain rattling as the palm of her hand connected. He spun with the force of the blow and his face slammed into the door of the toilet, before he collapsed to the floor with an incomprehensible *nnnnnngh,* and lay there unmoving.

Francine surveyed her handiwork with pride for a second, the result of years of training never used in real-world situations, seemingly just waiting for this moment. Who would have thought that, after forty years of attending and then teaching classes, she would finally find a use for it. Her instincts had kicked in and her movements had been automatic. She debated taking her phone out to snap a photo to show her classes, but thought better of it. She stepped around the prone figure on the floor and turned the key in the door. 'Gregor, it's me, Francine.'

She pulled the door open and Gregor almost fell out, narrowly missing the body on the floor. He looked around, confused. 'Jeez-o, what hit him?'

'Me,' Francine said, unable to keep the note of pride from her voice.

'With what? A battering ram?'

'This.' She held up her hand, demonstrating. 'Krav Maga.' Gregor shook his head, still trying to comprehend what had happened. 'It's a martial art. You know, like ju-jitsu or karate, but more dangerous.'

Gregor peered down at the man on the floor. 'Aye, I can see that. How do you…?' He gestured to Francine.

'I've done it for years. I still teach it a bit.' Gregor was looking at her, stupefied, so she expanded. 'Down at the leisure centre, and I teach a class at the Lodge. Sylvia's in it,' she said, helpfully.

Gregor looked horrified. 'You're teaching Sylvia *this*?' He gestured down at the young man on the floor, who was now snoring loudly. 'To *kill* people?'

Francine grinned. 'No killing involved, I promise. It's just tai chi down at the Lodge. It improves your wellbeing and reduces stress.'

Gregor groaned. 'I think I need a course of that right now. Is he dead?'

'Hardly.' The breathing of the man on the floor was laboured with whistles and clicks and a sort of snoring noise, but he was definitely alive. Francine carefully bent down to look at him; she was a little stiff after her adventure. 'He'll be asleep for a little while yet, though. Come on, let's get into that safe and then get out of here.'

55

PJ could hear an insistent buzzing and reached out an arm to flap away the bee that was circling around his head. His arm fell back down and he slapped himself in the face in the process. The buzzing stopped and then started again. PJ lifted his head. Ouch. Every part of it ached, and the slightest movement made him feel sick. He lay with his eyes shut for a few more rounds of buzz/no buzz and then tried to sit up once again. This time, he was more successful, although the effort caused the room to swim around him. Where was he? He closed his eyes again and lay back down until the spinning stopped.

Of course. He was inside the bookies. What the fuck had happened? He looked at his watch. It was just after four in the morning. He had a vague memory of something important that he had to do at half past three. Shite. He bolted upright – a mistake. He vomited all down himself and his face and head throbbed and pounded even more. He was supposed to leave the bookies by half past three, having… having done… what? That was it. He had to open the safe and empty it of all the cash it contained.

He staggered to his feet, drops of blood, apparently from his nose, now joining the vomit down the front of his black jacket. The buzzing started up again but he ignored it. He made his way to the office. Someone had thoughtfully opened the safe for him; that was kind. Actually, two safes, both of them open. He shut his eyes and opened them again; just one safe. Now all he had to do was reach in and take the money. He staggered over to the safe and put his hand in.

Nothing. He felt around inside. Still nothing. He used the torch on his phone to look inside. A big fat nothing.

Groaning, he collapsed onto the sticky carpet of the office and took out his phone. He groaned again. Fifty-six missed calls from Grinder. The buzzing had been explained. As he lay on the carpet, he formulated in his head the story of the six big men in balaclavas, the three he had bravely wrestled to the ground before they all set about him, and how he'd fought courageously to keep the safe full of takings from them, but how they had eventually tortured the code for the safe out of him and left him for dead. Yep, sounded good. Gratefully, he went back to sleep.

56

FRANCINE AND GREGOR HAD TOLD THE STORY three times already to an enthralled Sylvia and Harriet. All four of them were clasping huge glasses of whisky. When the novelty of the exciting story had worn off and Francine had demonstrated her Krav Maga moves for the fourth time, they all turned and gazed at the big bag stuffed with cash that lay on the table in front of them.

'Now what are we going to do with it?' Francine's voice was reverent.

Harriet pulled out a stack of twenty-pound notes and ran her thumb along the edge. 'Now we need to convert it to bitcoin.'

'An' how does that happen? This mining thing you told us about? Is it elves?'

Harriet laughed and patted Sylvia's hand. 'No, dear. We need to exchange the cash; I thought I might go along to a community meetup.'

Sylvia took a large swig from her glass and belched. 'Community meetup? That sounds like some sort of swingers' club.'

'Nothing like that at all. It's a bit geeky, if you must know.'

Francine sniffed. 'Geeky or not, if you think we're letting you head off to meet strangers with a bag full of cash, then you're very much mistaken.'

Harriet pushed her glasses up her nose. 'I've thought of that. I thought we could tell Jake we got a cash donation and get him and a couple of his lovely biker friends to come along with me.' She beamed. 'And that means I can get another go on his motorbike.'

57

Sylvia was knitting, quietly singing a Ramones medley to herself. It was her way of clearing her head to think. She could forget about the money, at least. Jake had come to collect Harriet for her meeting with the Crypto Elves and soon the cash would be tucked away somewhere inside a mountain that contained money that didn't actually exist, and Sylvia had just had to go with the flow on that one. No matter how many times Harriet explained it to her, all she could see in her mind were creatures from *Lord of the Rings* guarding a big pile of nothing. No, the money was dealt with, now they needed to decide what they were going to do with Fergus Lamont. It had been Gregor's turn to look after him today, but he was sleeping off last night's excitement and the stiffness from being squeezed into the cupboard at the bookies for over four hours, so Lamont was still at Francine's. *She* didn't seem to be suffering any ill effects from her athletic display; in fact, she seemed energised and with a spring to her step.

Lamont had so far refused to sign the document they'd had drawn up by one of the Lodge's residents who'd been a lawyer and still paid her annual fee to the Law Society of Scotland so that she could carry out pro bono work for her family, friends and neighbours. The document, if Lamont signed it, would finalise the sale to the residents of Janus Lodge and, so far, no amount of persuasion, cajoling and threats of violence had made him see sense. Even talk of crochet hooks hadn't had the desired effect. Sylvia was willing to go for *actual* crochet hook use, but the others were reluctant.

There was a brief rap at the door. Sylvia continued knitting furiously, frowning as she focused on the intricate pattern she was following. 'Come in! It's open!' She heard footsteps coming up the hallway – too fast for Harriet with her stick, too light for Gregor. It would be Francine. Without looking up from her knitting, Sylvia continued. 'How's that wee arsehole doing?'

'What wee arsehole would that be, Mrs Abercrombie?'

Sylvia dropped a stitch for the first time in years as her head snapped up. 'Who the fuck are you?'

'I think you know who the fuck I am, don't you?'

Sylvia glared at him. 'Not a clue. Some wee fanny in a suit, by the look of it.' She looked him up and down from head to toe and groaned. 'The *worst* type of fanny, no less; one that wears his suit and dress shoes with no socks. Minging. Just imagine all those bacteria multiplying in there, and it'll be hell on that leather. You off clubbing? Bit old for that, I would have thought.' She turned back to her knitting, trying to hold her hands steady so he wouldn't realise how scared she was. It wasn't working, so she put her hands back down in her lap again and glared at him. 'Oh, wait, I do recognise your face. I think it was on a poster in the window of Lidl. Didn't you nick an inflatable kayak, or something?'

'My name's Mahoney.'

'Aye, that's it, the inflatable kayak thief.'

Mahoney ignored her. 'I think you know one of my friends.'

'I do? That's a mistake; do let me know which one, I'll have to delete them from my Christmas card list.'

'One of my very dear friends. Who appears to have gone missing.'

'Are you sure he's not just avoidin' you? I would.'

Mahoney tweaked up the knees of his trousers and crouched down in front of her, putting a hand on either arm of her wheelchair. 'Fergus Lamont. Where is he?'

'Who?' Sylvia looked straight into his eyes and held back a shudder. They were as pale and cold as those of a horned viper she'd once seen on a nature programme. 'Oh, Thomas and Ailsa's boy, you mean? How would I know where he is? Have you asked them? They live just along the hall; they never go out, so you could go and see them. I'm sure they'd be delighted to chat with a man of your sartorial elegance.'

He remained crouching where he was, the unpleasant smile fixed in place. 'The police seemed to think you'd seen him on the day he disappeared.'

Sylvia scoffed. 'The polis? Since when can anyone believe anything *they* say?'

'True, true… but in this case, I happen to believe they were right.'

Sylvia leaned forward in her chair; it took all her courage to move closer to those reptilian eyes. 'I'll tell you what I told them, then. Which was that I hadn't seen hide nor hair of him an' they left believin' me. They even took a look all around my flat.' That was stupid. Sylvia wished she could have taken that back.

'That was a good idea. I'll have to do that myself before I go.' He didn't move, however. Sylvia's hands twitched in her lap, and she felt the wool and knitting needles beneath them. She should just take a needle and shove it in one of those snake-like—

'I wouldn't if I were you, Mrs Abercrombie.' Mahoney reached out and gently removed the wool and needles from under her hands. His fingers were as cold as his eyes and felt reptilian too – warm, dry and scaly – and her own fingers curled away from them in disgust. He stood up, his knees cracking after crouching in front of her chair for so long. 'I'll go and take a look for any signs of Fergus, shall I?'

Sylvia stared stonily back at him, feverishly trying to remember if she'd tidied away all signs of Lamont's presence. She nudged her hand over to her pocket, to see whether her mobile was there. While Mahoney was looking around the flat, she could phone someone. But the phone was over on the sideboard. Her chair was quiet; she'd maybe have time to get to it while he was looking around. However, it was as though he could read her mind. 'I'll just take you with me, I think; I wouldn't want you to do anything stupid.'

He put his hands on the back of her chair and spun her round. 'I can do it myself, you know. I've been in this chair a long, long time and I'm perfectly capable.'

'I'm sure you are, Mrs Abercrombie, but I'll do it, if you don't mind.'

'Well, I do mind, actually.' But he ignored her and pushed her chair into the bathroom and then into both of the bedrooms, briefly leaving her chair in the doorway of each to walk around the room, opening the wardrobes and bending down to glance under the beds in both rooms. Sylvia was relieved to see that there was no sign of Lamont anywhere, other than a water bottle with a straw in it on the bedside cabinet in the spare room. Nothing to raise Mahoney's suspicions.

She crossed her arms and glared at him. 'Happy, now?'

'What do *you* think?'

'Well, he's clearly no' here. So I'd be grateful if you'd get the fuck out of my flat. An' don't bother coming back. You're no' welcome. Neither you nor your wee pal, Lamont, when he eventually turns up from wherever he's slunk off to.'

Mahoney didn't respond, simply wheeled her back into the living room where he hesitated, his hands still on the back of her wheelchair. He then started to push her chair over to the patio doors.

'Where are you taking me?'

'Shut up. We're just going outside for a moment.'

'I don't want to go outside.'

'Well, we're going. And you'd better keep your mouth shut when we do. If you shout out, then the first nosey old bastard who pokes their head out to see what's happening will get this, understand?' *This* was something hard, pushed in between her shoulder blades. Sylvia wasn't sure if it was a gun, but she nodded. She couldn't take the risk. 'Good. I don't want to put something over your mouth because that would look suspicious if we meet anyone, so if we do, I just want you to smile and nod, right?'

Sylvia nodded again. She didn't mention that the very fact that a complete stranger was in charge of her wheelchair would look suspicious to anyone who knew her. Mahoney slid open the patio doors and poked his head out, looking left and right, before wheeling her smartly down towards the driveway. There was nobody about, and before she could consider what was the best course of action to take, Mahoney had wheeled her down the driveway and around the bend to where a Mercedes was waiting out of view of Janus Lodge.

Two thugs in flammable nylon shell suits, one fat, one skinny, were leaning against the car. As Mahoney appeared with her, they both stood up straight, staring from her to Mahoney.

Before any of them could say anything, Mahoney's phone rang. He pushed Sylvia's wheelchair over towards the skinny one. He had two black eyes and a big cut over the top of his nose. 'Here, put her in the back of the car with a blanket over her. I've got to take this. It's that arse from the Planning Department at the council.' He answered the call and put the phone to his ear. 'Hold on.' He stabbed at the mute button on the phone and started to walk off down the driveway, then stopped and turned round. 'She's got a smart mouth on her. If she gives you any bother, stuff something in it. Then bring the car down to the end of the driveway and meet me there.' Sylvia opened her mouth to call out, only to find a big, meaty hand clasp her face and cover her mouth. The hand tasted of sweat and stale cigarettes.

The big one picked her up out of her wheelchair as though she was a rag doll and thrust her into the back seat of the car, shoving her head into the leather of the seat.

Sylvia struggled to get up. 'Lie down,' Mahoney's henchman growled, 'and stay down.'

'No chance, you wee wank. You're no' takin' me anywhere.'

The skinny one suddenly came to life. 'We'd better tie her up, Dec.'

'What with?' Keeping one huge hand on Sylvia to hold her down, the big lump cast about for something to tie her up with.

Sylvia started to panic. She couldn't let them take her away. 'Get the fuck away from me, you mouth-breathing amoeba.' She opened her mouth wider to cry out, but the big one noticed and hit her face with the back of his hand, sending her head thudding into the back of the seat.

The skinny one punched him in the arm. 'Here, Dec, that's no' nice. You wouldn't want someone doin' that to your nana, would you?'

The Dec one shrugged. 'My nana's an arsehole too, so aye, ah would. We cannae drive wi' her like this. Open the boot.'

The skinny one scurried around to the back of the car and, just as easily as he'd picked her out of the chair, the hulking lout picked her out of the back of the car and carried her to the boot, one hand over her mouth to stop her from making a noise. His breath smelled of pear drops, but not in a pleasant way. Sylvia flailed her head and arms as much as she could, her useless legs no help to her at all.

'Here.' The skinny one held out a blanket and an oily rag. 'Wrap her up in this so she cannae move, an' shove this in her mouth.' They wrapped her expertly in the blanket and Dec placed her unceremoniously into the boot, which was otherwise empty, bending her legs at the knees to fit her in. Her arms were tight to her sides and she began to realise how Lamont must feel in his rubber prison. The oily rag was thrust into her mouth and the boot lid was firmly shut, leaving her in the dark.

She could hear muffled voices outside. 'What do we do with the wheelchair?'

'The boss didnae say nothin' about that. Just leave it. Come on. He'll kill us if we're not there to pick him up.'

Sylvia heard car doors slam and then felt a jolt as the car set off with a throaty roar.

58

As Jake slowed down at the bottom of the driveway of Janus Lodge, with Harriet tucked behind him on his motorbike, a Mercedes pulled out at speed, causing him to have to swerve to avoid it. He swore under his breath and glared at the driver, a skinny young man, and at the older man in the passenger seat who glared back. There looked to be a third person in the back seat, but Jake couldn't see him properly. He stopped the bike briefly, to make sure that Harriet was alright, and she gave him the thumbs-up.

Jake turned the bike into the driveway and drove slowly, cautious in case there were any other cars about. As he neared the bend, he saw something lying in the neatly cut grass at the side of the gravel drive. He stopped and swung himself off the bike, lifting Harriet off and putting the kickstand down in one fluid movement. With his hand under Harriet's elbow to steady her, they walked over to the object on the verge.

'That's Gran's wheelchair.'

Harriet gasped and put a hand to the helmet she was still wearing. 'It is! Oh no! Where is she?' The blackthorn hedge at the side of the drive was thick and impenetrable and there was clearly nowhere for anyone to disappear into it.

Jake glanced back down the driveway. 'That car! Did you see who was inside it?'

Harriet made a face. 'I saw the passenger. I can't be sure but… I think he was the man who wants to buy the Lodge. I saw him in Lydia's office one day. He's not a nice man.'

'I think he's got Gran.'

Harriet gasped again. 'What are we going to do?'

'Can you get back up to the Lodge on your own?' Jake moved over to his bike. 'I'm going to go and find her.'

Harriet held out a hand. 'But you can't! How will you know where they've gone?'

Jake shrugged. 'They turned left. I'll start from there.' He swung his leg back over the bike. 'Will you be okay?'

'Wait!' Harriet grabbed at his arm. 'LOC-8-OR.'

Jake nodded. 'Locate her? Gran? Of course we want to locate her. That's what I'm going to try and do.'

Harriet clutched at his arm even tighter. 'No, we've been playing hide-and-seek to take our minds off things. She couldn't get the wristband off. She's still got it on.' Jake looked even more confused. 'Look, it's a device that'll help us find her. Take me up to my patio doors so I can get the other bit of it, and while I'm doing that, call your granddad and ask him to meet us at mine straight away.' Jake hesitated, looking down the drive. 'I promise you. It's the only way we'll find her. They'll be too far away by now.'

59

THE THREE MEN IN THE CAR WERE silent. PJ was hunched over the steering wheel, concentrating. It was a luxurious car, very quiet, apart from the sound of banging coming from the boot. PJ glanced at Grinder and turned the radio on.

Grinder swore and turned it off again. 'What did you put her in the boot for?'

Declan leaned forward from the back seat. 'She was causing trouble, boss. Couldn't trust her in the back seat. Besides.' He looked hurt. 'She called me a mouth-breathing amoeba.'

Grinder turned to glare at him. 'Well, you *are* a mouth-breathing amoeba. Dear God, she's got to be nearly a hundred years old and she's a cripple. How much trouble could she cause us in the back seat? Listen to that banging. As soon as we get into town and have to stop at traffic lights, everyone around will know there's someone in there.' The banging continued. 'Stop the car, PJ.' PJ did as he was told and the car purred to a stop at the side of the road. There were few cars on the road leading away from Janus Lodge. 'Get her out of the boot and into the back seat where she's not going to make as much noise. Declan'll deal with her.'

Grinder sat stony-faced in the passenger seat as PJ and Declan got out and walked towards the back of the car. 'PJ?'

'Aye, what is it?' PJ paused with his fingers on the button that opened the boot.

'What *is* a mouth-breathing amoeba?'

60

Jake sped along the quiet roads, Harriet behind him, clutching onto him with one arm. Her other hand was in front of her, up against Jake's back, checking the digital display of the small screen on the LOC-8-OR unit she was holding. She had her iPad in its sleeve tucked down the front of her jacket. She spoke to Jake via the built-in intercom system on the bike's helmets. 'Left at the next junction. They've changed direction and it looks as if they're now heading into Glasgow.' She spoke slightly louder. The intercom was also linked to a mobile phone. 'Gregor… can you hear me?'

Gregor's voice crackled back into her helmet. 'Aye.'

'You got Google Maps up?'

'Aye, I think so.' Gregor's voice was hesitant and a little dubious.

'Good. Looks like we're heading into town.'

Jake nodded, his eyes firmly on the road as he took the bends. 'We'll hit the A814 soon. Hang on, we're coming up to a straight stretch.'

Harriet continued looking at the LOC-8-OR screen, but with her other arm she pulled herself in tighter to Jake as he speeded up.

The motorbike allowed Jake to get through the build-up of traffic at the Kingston Bridge and he turned off onto the Clydeside Expressway towards Clydebank. 'That's us on the A814 now, Gregor.' Harriet looked down at her LOC-8-OR. 'They're just turning into South Street. By the Clyde.'

Jake said, 'There are loads of warehouses and workshops down there.'

'Gregor – Jake says there are lots of warehouses and workshops down that bit. We could be heading for one of those. Have a look and see if there's anything obvious registered to Mahoney down that way.'

'Aye. Do you want me to call the polis?'

Jake shook his head. 'No, let's wait until we know exactly where they've taken her. We don't want to spook them and have them running off somewhere else.'

Gregor's voice was subdued. 'Be careful. But… find her.'

61

THE INTERIOR OF THE WAREHOUSE WAS STACKED with pallets and boxes – TVs, mobile phones, laptops, cases of drink, cigarettes – anything and everything by the look of things. Sylvia guessed that none of it was legitimate. They sat her in an uncomfortable plastic chair in the middle of all the pallets. She was shaky and felt dishevelled from being carted around in the blanket.

Mahoney stood in front of her, reflectively rubbing the puckered knife scar on his chin. She'd learned that the skinny man was called PJ. He was sitting on a box that, according to the packaging, contained a washing machine. Declan was leaning against a wall, idly lifting a dumbbell, a sulky look on his face.

Sylvia looked around her once more. 'This place could do wi' a wee tidy. You bring me here 'cause you need a cleaner?' Her voice cracked slightly, but she was determined not to show any fear. She nodded her head towards one of the pallets. 'You got receipts for all this lot?'

'You're rather annoying, Mrs Abercrombie, aren't you?'

'Aye, so my ex-husband always tell't me. But you don't need to listen to me; you could just let me go if you don't want me here.'

'Ah, but we *do* want you here. Well, we *need* you here, and you know why, don't you?' Sylvia remained silent. 'We need to know where Lamont is, that's all. You tell us that and we'll take you back to the old folks' home.'

'It's not an—'

Mahoney interrupted her. 'Just tell us where he is.'

'I've told you – I dinnae ken. Besides, don't you have other things to be worrying about right now?'

Mahoney narrowed his eyes. 'What do you mean?'

Sylvia inspected her nails. 'Well, a little bird told me that you lost a packet recently; that one of your bookies got held up.'

Mahoney looked over at PJ. 'And how would you know that? It's not made the news yet, I don't think.'

Shite. She hadn't been able to resist taunting him, but perhaps it had been a mistake. 'It's just up the road.' She shrugged. 'Maybe the postie tell't us.' She sighed. 'Who knows, my memory's not as good as it once was. Lot taken, was it?' She turned to face PJ. 'That where you got that face? They look sore, those bruises, big gang was it?'

PJ nodded, unable to stop himself. 'Aye, six of them.'

'Six of them? Big fellas, were they?'

'Aye, they—'

'Shut it, PJ.' Sylvia turned back to face Mahoney. '*You* don't know anything about it, do you, Mrs Abercrombie?'

She scoffed. 'Me? Do I look like a big fella?'

Mahoney frowned across at PJ. 'Maybe they weren't as big as PJ here thought.'

62

Francine sat in the easy chair in her living room, a cup of tea on a small table next to her, knitting in hand. As she knitted, she was chatting away, seemingly to herself. 'I told them to come round at three o'clock, I hope that's okay.' She paused and took a sip of her tea. 'I'm baking a cake for all of us. Lemon drizzle; I thought that would be nice. Do you like lemon drizzle?' She didn't wait for a response. 'Of course you do, everyone likes lemon drizzle cake, don't they?'

She smoothed out her knitting and held it up, admiring her own work. 'I'm sorry I've had to leave that… thing in your mouth and the mask on. I know that… some of my colleagues allow you to talk, but I'm going to keep it like this for a wee while if that's alright with you.' She turned her knitting around, still holding it up. 'I know you can't see this but it's a cardigan, and rather fine work, if I do say so myself. It feels strange to be knitting for me again after those months of frantic knitting for others.' She put the knitting down, suddenly all business again. 'Now, before they get here, we need to discuss this whole situation, don't we?'

She looked over at her guest. 'It must be nice for you to be out of that bed for once.' Fergus Lamont, still wearing his rubber sleep sack and the ball gag, was sitting meekly on the sofa opposite Francine. The gimp mask had been replaced by a tea towel showing the attractions of the Isle of Wight. The joys of The Needles and Osborne House had been rather spoiled by the patches of bright red blood that were slowly turning darker as they dried. 'I'm very sorry about… *my colleague* punching you in the nose like that. Still, at least it appears to have stopped bleeding now. Would you like me to take out those toilet paper plugs and see?' Lamont nodded slowly. Francine reached across, lifted the bottom of the tea towel and gently pulled both plugs out of his nostrils. 'There we are. That's better. Now, if I take that thing out of your mouth, do you promise not to shout?' Lamont nodded once more. Francine wasn't sure whether to believe him or not. She hesitated and stood up and walked over to a shelf of CDs. 'Let's see. Something fairly light, I think. How about *The Nutcracker*?' Lamont winced. 'I'm sorry; maybe not after what my colleague threatened to do.' She turned back to the shelf. 'Here. This one's perfect. Haydn's *Clock Symphony*; it's one of my favourites. I particularly love the second movement, the Andante.'

Francine inserted the CD into the player she insisted on keeping, despite Harriet's insistence that she should just stream her music, whatever that meant. She liked the shiny discs and the comforting snap as they locked into place and the whirr as the player started up. The music started quietly and she stood, appreciatively, taking in the dark, quiet opening of the start of the first movement and then going back to sit down as the music burst into its lively Presto. That would mask any sounds even if Lamont did make any noise. She doubted that her closest neighbours would be able to distinguish a cry for help from a French horn.

She moved her chair closer to Lamont and patted his rubber-clad hand, before putting her hands up to loosen the ball gag. 'Now, Fergus, you promised me. I wouldn't want to bring my colleague back in, would I?' Lamont whimpered faintly and she undid the buckle. As it came loose, Lamont stretched out his mouth, as if glad to be free of the impediment, which, she had no doubt, he was. 'A wee cup of tea?' Lamont gave her a hoarse 'Yes please' in response and she poured him a cup from the teapot. 'It should still be hot. Would you like milk? Or lemon?' Lamont shook his head, so she put the cup to his lips and he drank deeply. 'Oh goodness, you *are* thirsty. Here, I'll pour you another one.'

After Lamont had drunk his fill, Francine sat back down. 'Now, my colleague explained the problem to you. Your nasty friend has taken *our* dear friend Sylvia – Mrs Abercrombie – so we now need to come up with a plan to get her back, and that's where you come in.'

'And then will you let me go?' Lamont's plaintive voice was still hoarse but not quite as much as before.

'Oh, I'm sure we will, but we just need a wee bit of information about where he might have taken her.'

'But I… how? I don't…'

'We thought you'd perhaps have an idea about where he might have gone.'

Lamont cleared his throat. 'He's got… all sorts of properties… he could be anywhere.'

'Ah, well, we do know that he's somewhere along the Clydeside.' Harriet needed help pinpointing exactly where on the Clydeside it was. Her contraption, while accurate, was unable to establish exactly which building Sylvia might be in, and they didn't want to arouse suspicion by gaining entry into the wrong one, nor did they want to waste the time. Hence the request Harriet had relayed to Gregor. 'Do you know of any buildings along the Clydeside that this Mr Mahoney owns? A warehouse, or a workshop, or something of that nature?'

Lamont thought for a moment. 'I'll tell you if you let me go.'

Francine sighed. 'It doesn't quite work like that, dear. No; how it works is that you tell me which building it is, and then, if we get Sylvia out safely, *then* we let you go.' She hesitated. She couldn't lie to the poor man. 'After you've signed that little document, of course.'

'I can't… I can't… Mahoney is…' He drifted off, miserably.

Francine squeezed his arm. 'He's not a very nice man, is he?' Lamont shook his head. 'And he's already double-crossed you, as they say in the films, hasn't he?' Lamont nodded. 'So, quite frankly, I don't think you've got anything left to lose, have you?' Lamont's head remained still. 'And you've got quite a lot to win, you know, if you help us.' She looked at her watch. 'Talking of which, it's nearly three o'clock and thus time for this little meeting we've arranged, so if you could let me have the information we want, we'd be very grateful.'

'What… what happens if you *don't* get her out safely?' Lamont's voice quavered.

'Let's not think about that for now.' Francine patted his hand again and crossed her fingers.

63

Sylvia shifted uncomfortably in the chair as best she could. She wasn't used to being out of her own specially adapted wheelchair or furniture for so long. Plus, she was getting tired. Mahoney was pacing the floor in front of her. 'So, Mrs Abercrombie, things aren't going very well here. When you arrived, we only needed one piece of information from you, and now we need two.' He stopped his pacing and moved closer. 'Where is Fergus Lamont and where is my money?'

Sylvia glared up at him. 'And the answers are: how would I fucking know and how the fuck would I know. There, that do you?'

PJ stepped closer. 'Want me to do the usual, boss? Tie her up an' that?'

Mahoney gave a humourless cackle. 'Look at her, PJ. I don't think she's going to give us any trouble, is she? Pathetic old cow.'

Sylvia counted to ten in her head and clasped her hands in her lap, digging her fingernails into her palms. She glanced down at the watch on her wrist. She'd been here for half an hour or so, and it would probably be ages before anyone noticed that she was missing: Gregor was sleeping off the night's excitement, Francine was babysitting Lamont, and Harriet was off with Jake to see about turning the money into fresh air. Harriet. Sylvia glanced down at her other wrist. The wee light on the LOC-8-OR was still on. They'd realise she was missing at some point, and Harriet would know what to do. She relaxed a little; all she needed to do was to keep this wee wank talking, play for time.

Mahoney pulled another of the scabby plastic chairs up in front of her and sat down, his knees almost touching hers. He leaned forward. 'Now, Sylvia, let's start with Lamont. Where is he?'

Sylvia waved a hand in front of her face. 'Jeez-o, what have you been eating? And, by the way, it's Mrs Abercrombie to you.'

Mahoney's face twitched. 'Where. Is. Fergus. Lamont?'

'Oh, Fergus? Fergus *Lamont*? Is that who you mean? Why didn't you say so? Last time I saw him he was lying on my spare bed, all cosy in a rubber sleeping bag, looking like a shiny slug.'

PJ gave a wheezing laugh. Grinder glanced over at him and the laughing stopped immediately. PJ casually inspected his nails. 'Come now, Sylvia, you don't expect me to believe something quite so far-fetched, do you? I saw your flat. He wasn't there.'

Sylvia shrugged. 'No? Oh well, I must have seen that in a film, then.' She glanced upwards, pretending she was lost in thought. 'Oh, wait, this Lamont... did he have *love* tattooed on the knuckles of one hand and *hate* on the other?' Mahoney looked puzzled. 'Oh, naw, that was Robert Mitchum in *Cape Fear*. Sorry, wee man, I can't help you then. My mind, you know; I'm a pathetic old cow right enough.' She sat back in the chair and crossed her arms, glaring at him.

Mahoney thrust his chair back and stood up, pacing the room. 'Declan, stop messing about with those dumbbells; you're annoying me. Fetch me a bottle of whisky from one of the boxes over there.'

PJ nodded excitedly. 'You gonnae try and get her drunk, boss? So she'll tell you?'

'Don't be ridiculous. It's for me.'

Declan lumbered over to a pallet in the far corner of the room and opened one of the boxes, pulling out a bottle. He brought it over to Mahoney, who opened it up as though he were ripping Sylvia's head off and took a swig. Sylvia tutted. 'Straight from the bottle? That's not the way to treat a 14-year-old Balvenie Caribbean Cask.' He scowled at her. 'I prefer a 16-year-old Lagavulin masel' – nice and peaty – but that one's no' bad if you like your single malts fruity.'

Mahoney sat back down. 'Where's our money?'

Sylvia sighed dramatically. 'This again? I tell't ya. Do I look as though I could rob a bookies?'

He leaned forward, so close that the whisky on his breath stung her eyes. 'Well, somebody you know could, I'm sure of that. And if you don't start talking soon and tell us where Fergus Lamont is *and* where our money is, then not only will *you* suffer, but the people you love will, too. So, if I were you, Sylvia, I'd tell us sooner rather than later.'

'It's Mrs Abercrombie to you, ya wee wank.' Sylvia pulled back a fist and punched him on the nose.

64

As Harriet pointed, Jake slowly approached the warehouse, stopping his motorbike a short distance away. 'Francine says this one's it, according to Gregor. Mahoney has a couple of places here, but this one's the closest to the LOC-8-OR signal.' She showed Jake and he nodded, and turned off the engine.

The warehouse was an anonymous single-storey, red-brick building with a grey sheet metal roof and a wide roller-shutter door at the front, firmly closed. There was no sign outside. A high metal fence surrounded the place, but the gate was open. Weed-covered concrete led around to the side of the building. Jake raised the visor of his helmet. 'I can't see his car. He must have parked round the side.' The area was quiet and secluded. Cars passed along South Street, but Mahoney's industrial unit was tucked away behind a couple of others, all of which looked uninhabited at present. The River Clyde couldn't be seen, but a large crane and fancy apartments signalled its presence nearby.

Jake helped Harriet off the bike. Without her stick she wasn't particularly steady on her feet, and he held firmly onto her arm. 'I think we need some help.'

65

SYLVIA WAS NOW SLUMPED IN THE PLASTIC chair, heavy-duty bungee cords wrapped around her, holding her in place and ensuring that she couldn't move her arms. A thin trickle of blood ran down the side of her face from her left temple, where Mahoney's ring had caught her as he'd backhanded her. She cautiously raised an eyelid, pleased to see that Mahoney was in a worse state than she was. Her punch had caught him firmly on the mouth, splitting his lip open. Blood was spattered down the front of his shirt and his fancy jacket. She closed her eye again and pretended to be out for the count.

'Did you kill her, boss?' PJ's voice was a reverent whisper as he held a cloth to Mahoney's face.

'Of course I didn't. Hardly touched her. But I fucking will next time.' Mahoney's words were hard to make out as he struggled to speak without moving his lips. 'Get a bottle of water and throw it in her face. Before I see to her, she needs to tell us where Lamont and the money are.'

PJ shuffled away and Sylvia readied herself for a face full of water. She hoped that the cavalry would arrive soon.

66

Ailsa and Thomas Lamont were sitting in the comfortable armchairs in Francine's flat. Francine had moved to sit next to Fergus on the sofa. All of them except Lamont were drinking tea and eating lemon drizzle cake off Francine's best china. An extra plate lay on the table, with a thick, moist slice of the cake on it. Fergus was still tucked into the rubber sleeping bag, and his head was still in the gimp mask. The ball gag was back in place.

Ailsa leaned over and tapped her son's rubber-clad knee. 'Well, it's been very nice having this little chat, Fergus. Hasn't it, Thomas?'

'Yes, dear. Your mother's right, Fergus. It's nice of you to make time to visit us for once.'

Francine grinned to herself. Ailsa nodded happily. 'Yes, we should do it more often, shouldn't we, Fergus?'

Lamont shook his head violently and Thomas frowned. 'Now, that's not nice. You'll upset your mother if you take that attitude.'

Francine topped up the teacups. 'I think Fergus understands, Thomas. We had a little chat before you came, and he's seen sense on this building nonsense and is going to sign the contract.'

Ailsa shook her head and her voice was a whisper. 'A brothel. I can't believe you were going to sell this place to build a brothel, Fergus.'

They all shook their heads and tutted, with the exception of Lamont, and then Francine smiled. 'But I think he's seen the error of his ways and has realised that this Mr Mahoney of his has led him astray. So, we won't have any more of that nonsense, will we, Fergus?' Fergus slowly shook his head. 'Or certain documents may find their way to certain people and certain information may find itself in the hands of certain other people. And you certainly don't want any of that to happen, do you?' Fergus shook his head more firmly. 'Good. Then I think we can safely take that ball gag off, don't you? And then you can have a nice little chat with your parents, now we've got all that nasty business stuff out of the way.'

Thomas looked at Ailsa and she raised her eyebrows back at him. 'Can Ailsa and I have it, Francine? That thing?'

67

Jake had carried Harriet over to a low wall and sat her on it, and was leaning against it, his arms crossed. Harriet was tapping away on her iPad and talking into her phone. A roaring of motorcycles in the distance became louder, and Harriet's voice was excited as she said into the phone, 'That's them here, Gregor. I have to go. I'll call you back soon, I promise.'

Harriet counted as twenty motorcycles turned into the side road and stopped at the end, easing into neat rows like a motorcycle version of the Red Arrows. Some of the bikes had passengers on the back. The bikers dismounted and walked over to where Harriet and Jake were waiting, taking off their helmets as they did so. All of them were wearing baby-blue balaclavas with red skull and crossbones knitted into the back. Several of them went over to give Harriet a hug and many of them slapped Jake on the back.

'What's the score, big man?' one of them said.

Jake nodded towards Harriet. She held out her iPad on which she'd drawn a plan of attack. The bikers clustered around Harriet. 'Jake's checked around the side for me. There's one door, halfway along the side, just here.' She pointed to the screen. 'Jake didn't try it, but we'll assume it's locked. Mahoney's car's parked around there, too. That needs to be disabled.' She tapped a button and the screen turned into a 3-D rendition which she spun around. 'There's a small window at the back, but that's the only one. I think it must lead to the office. It's too high and too small to get out of, Jake says.' The strategy map disappeared as she pulled up a floorplan. 'I found the unit on the website of a company dealing in industrial properties. Here.' She tapped a bent and arthritic finger on the screen. 'Office, toilets, kitchen and two large warehouse spaces. We don't know where they're holding Sylvia.' She tapped again and the map reappeared, this time covered with different coloured arrows and lines.

One of the bikers whistled. 'Man, that's cool. Where d'you get all this stuff from?'

'*Age of Empires*, *Call of Duty*, *Civilisation*, *Warcraft*… you know.' Harriet shrugged. 'We don't know where Sylv will be, so I need you to split up once you get inside. You'll need to be in four groups: green, red, blue, yellow, just like the map, and follow these arrows.'

'How many of them are in there?'

Jake spoke up. 'Three, we think. There were only three of them in the car as far as I could tell, but we don't know whether there were any others already here. There's no other vehicles about, though. Before we go in, we'll have a final recce, so go quietly for now. Ideally, we want to see if we can hear any voices, so we can work out exactly where she's being held. If they've got guns…'

He drifted off and Harriet squeezed his arm. She pushed her glasses up her nose. 'Hopefully there won't be anyone else and you can just swoop in and collect Sylvia. She… we don't know if they've hurt her.' For the first time, Harriet lost her poise and her voice hitched. 'And she hasn't got her wheelchair, so you'll have to carry her out. Be gentle with her, please.'

The bikers nodded. Jake divided them into groups and they inspected the map once more, to see where they needed to be once they were inside. Then they all put their helmets back on and walked slowly and quietly around the side of the building. Jake lingered to give Harriet a quick kiss on the top of her head. Harriet let out a shaky breath and clutched her iPad to her. She waited for the sound of the door being kicked in.

68

A FAINT BUZZING HAD STARTED IN SYLVIA'S head and the ground was swimming in front of her. She felt light-headed. She lifted her head. 'D'ya think I could have some water? Some actual water, to drink, no' thrown in my face like the last lot.'

Mahoney nodded at PJ, who scurried off back to the room over at the other side of the warehouse, which Sylvia assumed was a kitchen or an office. He came back with a chipped mug filled with water and held it out to her. The inside was stained with what she hoped was just tea. 'You need some bicarb on that; it's minging.' PJ simply thrust the mug closer. Sylvia lifted her hands as far as she could, which wasn't very far since her arms were restricted by the elastic cords binding her to the chair. 'You'll have to do the honours, unless your boss wants you to unwrap me from this chair.'

PJ looked over at Mahoney who touched a finger to his lip and winced. 'No, I most certainly do *not* want you to do that, PJ.' PJ shrugged and lifted the mug to Sylvia's mouth.

Much more gently than Sylvia was expecting, he held the back of her head and placed the mug against her lips, making sure that he wasn't pouring too much into her mouth at once. She took several gulps and smiled at PJ, feeling much better. 'Thank you, young man; I appreciate it.' He nodded as if faintly embarrassed and stepped back to his former position.

Mahoney sat on the chair in front of her once more. Sylvia bit back a grin as she noted that his chair was out of range of a punch now, although she clearly wasn't able to throw one anymore. His voice was weary. 'Do you have my money?'

'I do not.' It wasn't a lie.

'Do you know where it is?'

Sylvia shrugged. 'I think some elves in a mountain might have it.' Which also wasn't a lie, since it's exactly what she'd understood from Harriet's lecture on cryptocurrency. So far, so good; she would still be eligible for heaven.

Mahoney jutted his chin out and closed his eyes. 'For fucks— Fine; we'll leave that for the moment. Where is Fergus Lamont?' Sylvia remained silent. 'Look, we know he came to see you, and he hasn't been seen since. You as good as told me that you knew where he was. Why not make it easy on yourself and tell us? I'm not going to ask you again as nicely as this. The next time I ask will be painful.' Sylvia stared back at him. He didn't take his cold, hard snake eyes from Sylvia's face. 'Declan, fetch me the bag from the top of that pallet.'

Without turning her head, Sylvia could hear Declan lumbering away, breathing noisily as he did. Mahoney leaned forward. 'What happened to your legs, Mrs Abercrombie?'

Sylvia was taken aback. 'My legs? I was in a car crash, why?'

'Do you have any feeling in them at all?'

'Not really, no.'

His voice was calm and soft. 'Where does the feeling start?'

If he wanted to chat, that was fine; the longer she could delay telling him where Lamont was, the longer her rescuers would have to get to her. Her rescuers. Maybe there weren't going to *be* any rescuers. No, they would come. 'I was lucky. The injury was in my lumbar spine. L1. I have a wee bit of movement in my hips, but not much, and I have some sensation in the tops of my legs.'

Declan lumbered back over and held out a black and yellow bag. Mahoney leaned forward as he unzipped the bag, keeping his eyes on Sylvia's all the time. He pulled out a hammer. 'So, if I were to hit the tops of your legs with this hammer, it would hurt?'

69

FRANCINE RETURNED TO THE LIVING ROOM AFTER showing Ailsa and Thomas out and sat back down in her favourite armchair. 'There, that was nice, wasn't it, Fergus? It's not good for a child to be estranged from their parents like that; hopefully, you and your mum and dad can have a much healthier relationship now.' She looked at him reproachfully, even though he wouldn't be able to see her face. 'It would be good if you visited them more often; they miss you, you know. Can you promise me you'll do that in future?'

Lamont nodded. 'Would you… can you take this mask off me, please. It's so hot in here.'

'Oh dear, of course it's hot. I'm sorry.' Francine stood up again. 'I'm afraid that my old bones don't do well in the cold but that's just selfish of me. I'll turn the heating down and put another cardigan on.' Lamont whimpered and she patted his shoulder. 'I know, dear, but I promised… my colleagues… that I wouldn't take the mask off. It's better that you don't see all of us; it won't be for much longer now, I'm sure.' She hoped that would be the case, at least. Before she could sit back down, there was a soft tap at the door of her flat. Francine sighed and picked up the ball gag, which she'd managed to stop Ailsa from pocketing, and buckled it around his head. 'I'm afraid I need to put this back on you for a wee while. There. I'll be back in a minute and we can have some more tea and cake.'

Lamont's shoulders slumped. Francine closed the door to the living room behind her and opened her front door. Gregor slipped inside.

'I'm worried.' His voice was soft.

'What is it?' Francine kept her voice low, too. 'Have you heard anything?'

'No, not yet. Harriet said she'd update me once they'd found Sylv, but I'm worried Mahoney'll hurt her.'

'Well, what can we do? We can't do anything from here apart from looking after Fergus.'

'See, that's what I was thinking. Mahoney was looking for Lamont, right, when he came here?' Francine nodded. 'Well, why don't we let him speak to him?'

'Let Lamont speak to Mahoney, you mean?'

'Aye. It might buy us a bit more time, so that he doesn't hurt Sylv.' Gregor pulled a phone out of his pocket. 'I switched this off the day we… started looking after him. I've just turned it back on again. He's got loads of messages and missed calls.'

'I'm sure he has.' Francine considered what he was suggesting. 'Will the police be able to trace it?'

'I dunno. But we'll only leave it on until he's made the call and then turn it back off again. I'm sure it'll be fine. What do you think?'

'Can we trust him? Fergus, I mean. Can we trust him not to say anything about where he is?'

Gregor lifted his hands. 'I don't know. We seem to have convinced him that Mahoney's double-crossed him, and I'm sure we can make it worth his while not to speak.' Gregor pulled a toy gun out of his pocket. 'I picked it up off the swaps table. It's not convincing to look at, but with it held to your forehead… well…'

Francine frowned. 'What would we get him to say?'

'To tell Mahoney not to hurt Sylvia, that he's gone away for a wee while but will be back soon, to let Sylvia go… that sort of thing.'

Francine thought for a moment. 'Do you think we ought to run it past Harriet?'

'I don't want to waste any more time.'

Gregor sounded frantic and Francine nodded. 'Come on, then.' She opened the living room door and they went in and sat down.

70

SYLVIA COULDN'T TAKE HER EYES OFF THE hammer, polished steel with a curved claw at one end and a black rubber handle. It looked new and clean and heavy. Mahoney picked it up and slapped the weighted head onto the palm of his other hand as though he enjoyed the feel of it slapping against his flesh. She shuddered. She wondered how many times he'd done that in the past.

She didn't know what to do for the best. She couldn't tell him where Fergus Lamont was, because that would put the rest of them in danger. But she needed to give him something. The money. Maybe she could promise him the money from the robbery. She opened her mouth to speak, but the sound of a ringing mobile stopped her in her tracks, and she took her eyes off the hammer to look over to the source of the noise.

Mahoney had taken off his bloodstained jacket and put it on the pallet PJ was leaning on. PJ reached into the pocket of the jacket and pulled out the phone, his eyes widening as he looked at the screen. 'Boss?'

Mahoney was still looking calmly at Sylvia, the hammer still kissing rhythmically off the palm of his hand. 'Aye?'

'It's Lamont.' He held the screen towards Mahoney, his face full of excitement.

'Lamont?' Mahoney dropped the hammer and jumped up. 'Well, answer it, you prick.' He snatched the phone out of PJ's hand and swiped the screen upwards. 'Fergus, where the fuck are you?'

Sylvia gasped and managed to turn it into a cough. In the echoing space of the warehouse, she could just hear the voice on the other end of the phone. '*I'm fine.*'

'I didn't ask *how* you are, you prick. I asked *where* you are.'

'*I'm… I'm not sure exactly where I am.*' The voice was hesitant.

'You're not?' Mahoney looked quickly over at Sylvia. She stared straight in front of her, trying not to let all her feelings show in her face. 'Aren't you at that old people's home?'

Again, there was a pause before Lamont answered. '*I don't… I don't think so. No. I'm in a… bar.*'

'A *bar*?'

'*No! Wait! A barn. That's it, a barn… In the Highlands. Near…*' There was an extended moment of hesitation and the voice, when it came, sounded slightly confused. '*Trumpton.*'

'Trumpton? Where the fuck is Trumpton?'

Declan nodded knowledgeably. 'You know, boss, the kids' TV show: Chippy Minton the carpenter; Miss Lovelace that sold the hats; Mr Platt; Pugh, Pugh, Barney McGrew, Cuthbert, Dibble and Grubb. They were—'

Mahoney turned on him. 'Are you taking the fucking piss? You too, Fergus. What the—'

'*Not Trumpton, Plop… Plockton. That's it. It's a… village… prettiest village in Wester Ross.*'

Sylvia lowered her head. He was being coached by Gregor. Plockton had been one of their favourite places to visit as a family. The Jewel of the Highlands. Gregor must be writing notes to tell Lamont what to say; his writing had always been atrocious back then, and clearly still was.

Mahoney took the phone away from his ear and stared at it, his face thunderous. 'You're on holiday in some fancy Air-fucking-bnb barn in the middle of nowhere, and you've left me with all this shit?' Mahoney's face became even redder. 'Wait. Who's paying for this little holiday of yours? Is it the money from the bookies, you bastard?'

'*What?*'

'Did you fucking steal from me?' Mahoney started pacing like a caged lion. 'You're a dead man, Lamont.'

'*Steal from you? No! Oh my God… No! I wouldn't steal from you, Grinder, I swear.*' Lamont's voice sounded panicked. '*What do you mean, anyway, the money from the bookies?*'

'Did you rob my bookies? Springfield Road?' Mahoney's voice was calm and quiet, and about a hundred times more dangerous for that. Sylvia shivered.

'*The bookies has been…? God no! I don't… Who could…*' Lamont's voice speeded up. '*Listen, Grinder, I think I know—*'

There was a muffled rustling on the other end of the line. Sylvia knew it was her only chance and started to sing the chorus from The Ramones' 'I Wanna Be Sedated'. She sang it as loudly as she could. She'd managed to get two lines in before the phone went dead. Hopefully they'd heard her on the other end of the line. They would know she was here, even if they didn't know where 'here' was.

'Fuck!' Mahoney threw the phone at Declan. It bounced off his shoulder and landed on the floor, skittering to a halt under one of the pallets. 'Fuck!'

71

'YOU DIDN'T? TELL ME YOU DIDN'T?' LAMONT'S voice was a whisper.

Gregor took the toy gun away from his head. 'We told you, Fergus. We're connected. You don't want to mess with us.'

Lamont curled up into a ball as far as his rubber sheath would allow. 'Nonononononono. Oh my God. You don't know what you've done. Stealing from Mahoney…'

Gregor blew on the end of the fake gun and Francine shook her head at him. 'We're not afraid of Mahoney. Our boss is *way* harder.' He turned to Francine and mouthed, *Sylvia*.

'You don't know what you've done,' Lamont said once more, and then subsided into whimpers.

Gregor patted him on the shoulder. 'All the more reason to do as we say. Not just now, but afterwards. As far as anyone's concerned, you took a wee break in the Highlands to think things over. When you came back, you realised that selling Janus Lodge and making your parents homeless was just too cruel, so you're selling it to its residents for…' He turned to Francine. 'How much was it that we raised?'

'Three and a half million pounds, give or take.'

'That's right. So you're selling it to us for two and a half million, Fergus.'

'But that's…'

'That's right. It's very generous of you. We might even name the new wing we'll build with the rest of the money we raised the Fergus Lamont Wing, to say thank you.'

'But I—'

'And remember, Fergus, one peep out of you and those documents... well... not just those documents. There's also the proof that you stole all that money from the Springfield Road bookies.'

'But I... What proof?' The sweat was pooling on Lamont's top lip, the only part of his face that could be seen.

'Oh, don't you worry about that, Fergus. There'll be proof, I can assure you of that.' Gregor raised his shoulders and made a face at Francine. He had no idea what proof they could engineer, but the last few days had made him sure that the four of them could come up with something. He smiled again at Francine and she smiled back. They might not have accomplished everything they set out to do, but The Ramones had told them that Sylvia was still alive.

72

MAHONEY CONTINUED TO PACE FURIOUSLY. SYLVIA WAS feeling more confident that help was on the way. At first, when she'd heard Lamont's voice, she'd been worried that he'd managed to get free, somehow; but as the conversation had gone on, she'd realised that wasn't the case. She felt reassured.

PJ put his hand up, tentatively, as though he was a five-year-old on his first day at primary school who'd left it too late to ask to go to the toilet. 'Boss?' Mahoney didn't answer and PJ took it as his cue to continue. 'Does that mean she's had nothing to do wi' it? That Lamont just went off wi' the cash?' Mahoney didn't answer, simply kept up his pacing. 'Does that mean we should… let her go?'

Sylvia kept her head down, not daring to look up.

Mahoney turned on PJ. 'Let her go? You think we're just going to let her go?' He bent down to pick up the hammer from where he'd dropped it. 'Besides, I think all that nonsense about being in the Highlands was a ruse. I'm almost sure, now, that Lamont is at that place, and once we've seen to this old bag, we'll go and find him, even if we have to rip every one of those old bastards limb from limb.'

Sylvia couldn't stand it any longer. 'Oh why don't you go and stick your fucking—' Her words were drowned out by a loud banging in the first room she'd been brought through. It was almost identical to this one, filled with pallets and windowless, but without the roller door at one end.

PJ threw himself to the floor, covering his head and curling into a ball. Declan looked around him, his head turning from one side to the other like a baffled metronome. Mahoney disappeared from Sylvia's view in the direction of the roller door. There was the sound of running footsteps now, and loud voices. *'Toilets, clear.'* Another voice: *'There's the door to the other space!'*

Immediately after that, the metal door in the wall separating the two warehouse rooms burst open and five men wearing black leather and baby-blue woollen balaclavas burst in. 'She's here!' one of them cried out, and the room was soon filled with more of the leather-clad men and women. Sylvia spotted her grandson amongst them.

'Jake!' she sobbed, relief flooding her body. 'Oh, Jake!' He strode over and pulled at the bungee cord binding her, swearing under his breath as he did so. 'No! Leave me! Get Mahoney! The door!' She turned her head in time to see Mahoney over at the far end of the room. He'd inserted a key into a pad on the wall and the roller door was slowly moving upwards. Light flooded in from the gap that had been created. As Jake started to run his way, he pulled the key out and pressed a button and the door started to roll down again. Mahoney threw himself onto the floor and squeezed his way out through the narrow gap before it completely closed.

'Shit!' Jake started to run towards the door they'd come in by. 'He's getting away!'

73

Harriet was still perched on the wall, surrounded by motorbikes. There had been silence for a while as Jake and his friends reconnoitred the place, but for the last minute or so she'd heard huge amounts of banging and crashing. Harriet clutched her iPad to her, wishing she could go in and help. She was really worried about Sylvia.

A metallic clanking drew her gaze to the metal roller shutter set into the far side of the front wall of the building. The shutter moved slowly upwards a couple of feet and then slowly began to lower itself again. Hands and arms appeared in the gap. It wasn't Jake or his friends; Harriet could tell by the sleeves. Blue-and-white striped shirt sleeves, an expensive-looking watch. As a head and shoulders followed, Harriet recognised the man from the Mercedes – Mahoney. He hauled himself out and struggled to his feet as the roller shutter closed behind him.

He didn't look over to the wall where she was sitting, and ran around the corner, probably to get his car. He was brought up short, presumably by the sight of the four slashed tyres in Harriet's plan. He hesitated a moment and then turned round.

As he turned, he saw her. Harriet shrank back as far as she could on her wall. He looked like a madman. There was blood all over his face and his shirt, and his hair was wild. He hesitated a moment, as if weighing up his options, and then seemed to come to the conclusion that escaping into South Street was his best option. He took off running. This had all taken only about thirty seconds, and no one else had, as yet, appeared from the warehouse. He would get away and Harriet couldn't have that. She tried to jump down off the wall, but it was too high.

She began to panic and called out for Jake. Mahoney had to pass her wall in order to get out through the gate of the industrial unit. Harriet looked down at the iPad in her hands. She only had one chance to do this. She took aim, reminding herself that her prowess as a baseball pitcher had won her medals. She launched the iPad at Grinder's head. He grunted as it made a satisfying *thwack* when it met the side of his head, and he crumpled to the ground, motionless.

74

THE INSIDE OF THE WAREHOUSE WAS QUIET. Only random scufflings and muffled grunting indicated there was anybody there. The pallets piled with boxes containing everything from whisky to white goods and power tools to patio sets were still exactly where they had been. The only thing which had changed from an hour or so before was that Sylvia was no longer tied to the chair under the flickering strip light in the ceiling. Instead, there were three chairs, arranged in a triangle and facing outwards. The light still flickered and buzzed above them. In the chairs, bound, gagged, and looking utterly miserable, were Grinder Mahoney, PJ and Declan.

From outside, the sound of police sirens could be heard, getting closer and closer. Mahoney grunted and struggled in his bonds, desperately trying to free his hands and arms. All he succeeded in doing, however, was toppling his chair. He crashed to the floor with a muffled shriek, the fall breaking the crust on the lip that Sylvia had split earlier. Blood started gushing once more. The sound of the police sirens was joined by the screeching of tyres, the opening and slamming of car doors, and the sound of footsteps outside.

From his position on the floor, Mahoney's eyes were glued to the ribbon of light underneath the roller-shutter door. It was open about four inches at the bottom; not so much that a casual observer would notice in passing, but enough that anyone who had just pulled up outside in a police car, having been summoned by a mysterious phone call, would spot in a moment.

Shadows crossed and darkened the ribbon of light as Mahoney

watched, but then the ribbon grew to a thick band, and then a sheet, as the door rolled upwards and the space was taken up by six curious policemen. Mahoney groaned and closed his eyes.

The police officer at the front bent down and read the words on a piece of paper that had been carefully placed on the ground, just inside the door: *'Dear Police, you might want to check the contents of these pallets against your lists of stolen goods. Happy birthday, A Helpful Friend.'* The police officer stepped closer to Mahoney and crouched down in front of him. He grinned. 'Well, well, Grinder Mahoney, as I live and breathe. It looks very much as though yer tea's oot at long last, as my old gran would have said.'

75

THE SIGN OUTSIDE THE LODGE HAS BEEN revamped and now reads: 'Janus Lodge – Owned by its Residents'. Garlands of flowers hang in the hallway: thistles, lavender, roses, heather and bluebells, all beautifully knitted and crocheted in shades of purples, greens and whites. Organ music is coming from the communal lounge, a rather mixed bag of tunes that includes 1960s pop, country music and a medley of The Andrews Sisters. Clearly, someone is working their way through their repertoire.

The lounge, too, is decked out with flowers – some real, some knitted. The usual comfy chairs have been cleared away. Instead, rows of folding chairs have been placed on both sides of the room, each chair tied with a swag of filmy, violet organza. A passageway has been left from the door of the lounge to the front of the room, where a smartly dressed and pleasant-looking woman is standing, her hands folded, waiting expectantly.

The seats are filled with Janus Lodge's residents, all dressed in their finery. Francine and Harriet are sitting in the front row at one side, spruced up, made up, their hair blue-rinsed to within an inch of its life. Ailsa and Thomas Lamont are sitting over at the other side, holding hands. Lydia is directing operations from the back of the room, making sure everyone is comfortable. She looks out into the corridor and then ducks back into the room. 'They're coming!'

The organist, an elderly man in a shiny black suit, stops playing The Village People's 'YMCA' and launches into a spirited rendition of Mendelssohn's 'Wedding March'. The assembled guests all turn towards the back of the room.

Gregor appears at the door. He's wearing a kilt in the greens and blues of the Abercrombie tartan and a velvet doublet in rich, dark purple with shiny silver buttons. He hesitates slightly and then walks to the front of the room and shakes the hand of the woman standing there. He looks around as the door opens again and Jake, in matching kilt and doublet, appears at the door, holding it open for Sylvia in her wheelchair. It, too, is covered in flowers. Sylvia is wearing a lilac antique lace dress. Flowers from the Lodge's garden are entwined in her hair and she is carrying a bouquet of more of them. She smiles at Gregor and wheels herself to the front of the room, Jake at her side.

The wedding is over. Gregor and Sylvia make their way back down the aisle, hand in hand, as the residents who are able to, line the aisle, holding up a variety of dildos and vibrators to make a beautiful arch for the newlyweds to go under as they exit the room.

Acknowledgements

Huge thanks first of all go to Maxim Jakubowski, Editor-at-Large, who has always been really supportive of my writing; it's also good to know that at least one other person shares my sense of humour. And thank you so much to all the team at Bedford Square/No Exit Press, who have been an absolute joy to work with.

Sincere thanks and big love to everyone at my place of work, Glasgow Women's Library – especially GWL's lovely librarian, Wendy Kirk – and to the wonderful women who attend Story Café, for laughing when I read out parts of the book when it was a work in progress. And thank you also to Barry Ryan for reading the manuscript and telling me it was funny (even if you were indulging me, Barry, it's much appreciated)! Along the same lines, thank you, Facebook Chums, for your lovely responses to my posts about my actual visits to the inspiration for 'Janus Lodge'. Without the encouragement those responses provided, I may never have gone on to write *Knit One, Heist One*.

I couldn't have written the book without the support of my partner, Ewan, and for always being on hand with a cup of tea for me (he told me to emphasise that he can do more than just make cups of tea, because, apparently, that's all I ever give him credit for, but there you go).

And I am forever grateful to my Mum and Dad, Joyce and Patrick Moore, for giving me not only a love of books and stories, but also of comedy and fun.

About the Author

Donna Moore was born in 1962 and led a sheltered childhood in a small English village. A crime fiction fan from a young age, Donna wanted to be one of Enid Blyton's *Famous Five* and fight crime with the aid of only a basket of cucumber sandwiches and a bottle of ginger beer. She spent her spare time following mysterious strangers around the village - especially those with cockney accents and a couple of days' growth of stubble - until a complaint from the new local vicar put a stop to her sleuthing career.